Morrigan's Heirs

The Andovia Chronicles Book 4

Tiffany Shand

DEDICATION

For my mum, Karen.

ACKNOWLEDGMENTS

Editing Dark Raven Edits

Cover Design by Kristina Romanovic

MAP OF THE LOWER
R E A L M

Spirit
Grove

Crystal
Palace

ANDOVIA

ALARIS

Old City

VARDEN
FOREST

EREDEN

GLENTEL

N

NW NE

W E

SW SE

S

RING OF
SORROW

REALM OF THE
UNDERSEA

JORIAM

SLAVE
ISLANDS

DRAGON ISLANDS

URSAIA

DORINGA

CHAPTER 1

I don't see any guards." Nyx Ashwood motioned for her sister, Niamh, to follow her as they headed into the temple in the old city of Varden. She pushed her long pink plaited hair off her face. Her purple wings furled behind her like folding leaves. "Come on, let's look around and get out of here before anyone sees us."

"Why would there be guards here? The city is supposed to be abandoned." Niamh's long blonde hair fell over her face and her pointed ears stuck out.

"I told you I thought I heard minds in the city when we came here the other day. They disappeared before I had a chance to find them." She pushed her way through the double doors of the temple and kept her senses on alert. *I don't hear any minds or detect any presences here,* she told Niamh in thought. *But that didn't mean there was no one there. The guards could be shielded.*

A month had passed since they had stopped Lyra Duncan, the high priestess possessed by the former Queen of Andovia. Walking through parts of the abandoned city still sent chills down her spine.

"What are we looking for?" Niamh frowned.

"Anything that might give us an idea of how to save Ambrose." Nyx opened the door to Lyra's bedchamber.

A lot had happened since the former Queen of Andovia

had killed the Archdruid's wife and attempted to kill Nyx. Since then things in Andovia had been restless.

They went through the empty halls of the temple until they reached what had been Lyra's bedchamber. The large room had bare grey stone walls and a small bed covered with furs. A table and chairs were by the window and a large trunk stood on the other side of the room.

"Not much of a bedchamber for a former queen," Niamh remarked. "I still don't understand why she didn't get revenge on the Archdruid before now. If she has been in Lyra's body for the last century, why didn't she do anything to get back at him for taking her realm?"

"She told me she couldn't restore herself to her true body and couldn't use her full power in Lyra's body. That's why she needed me." Nyx shuddered. "She needed the blood of another mind whisperer."

"But how could that help?" Niamh's frown deepened. "Are we related to her?"

"Maybe we have a blood link. We could be her descendants." She found a large wooden chest at the end of the bed and rummaged through it. "The queen was the first mind whisperer, so…" She tossed aside the different linens and felt around the bottom of the chest, knocking on the side of it a panel opened. Sliding her hand inside the gap, her fingers closed around something metal and she pulled it out. It was a small gold round object. Like a large pendant. No, not a pendant — it was too large for that.

Niamh opened the door to the wardrobe and rummaged through cloaks and several robes. "It looks like someone has already been here. Are you sure this place is abandoned? We know Ambrose and the queen came here all the time."

"I guess the queen could have brought someone with her, but I doubt they would still be here." Nyx opened the object and light flared to life. A glowing image of a beautiful young woman with dark hair and large wings stood beside a red-haired man. Both smiled. Nyx gasped. "I think there's something in here."

Niamh didn't respond as she carried on rummaging through the wardrobe.

"Niamh, you need to see this."

Still her sister ignored her. "How many robes does one woman need? Gods."

"Niamh!"

"I'm busy. I can feel something at the back —"

"Niamh!" Nyx shouted at her.

"What?" Her sister pushed her long blonde hair off her face.

"Look at this." She held up the glowing image. "It's Ambrose, the queen and their children."

Niamh's eyes widened. "Is that… us?"

All three girls had blonde hair, blonde that flashed with different colours. One had large purple wings. All of them had pointed ears and the same blue eyes.

"No, that can't be us." Niamh shook her head. "Can it? It's impossible."

"The queen is supposed to be dead. Who are we to say what's impossible?" Nyx stared at the image harder. "It looks a bit like me — before Harland cut my ears." It had been so long since her former foster father had cut off her pointed ears that she barely remembered what they were like before.

"But that was a hundred years ago."

"That's us, me, you and Novia." She pointed to the different figures.

Niamh scowled at the mention of their other sister. "But… How? We can't be that old. I joined the Order when I was ten. You ended up in Joriam and I ended up in

Ereden. Wouldn't we be older? I doubt children stay that young for a century."

Nyx sighed. "Maybe we are her —"

"No, don't say it. Don't even think it. Our mother can't be that lunatic."

Nyx had never really thought about the possibility of the Andovian Queen being their mother, but in some ways it would make sense. Neither of them had any idea who their parents were.

"She is the only mind whisperer left. Come on, you must have considered we might be related to her."

Niamh shook her head. "She's mad and we're — maybe it's a trick. Maybe her daughters survived and one of them is our ancestor."

"Lucien tested our blood. He said we're triplets and we have druid and fae blood. Ambrose and the queen are the only druid and fae couple we know of."

"You're involved with a druid too," Niamh pointed out. "I don't want it to be true. If that woman is our mother, what does that make us?"

"It doesn't make us like her." Nyx squeezed her shoulder. "Maybe we should call Novia."

They hadn't seen their other sister for a while now since they had gone to stay with her on Glenfel Island.

"Why? She was so desperate to get back to her precious island prison." Niamh rolled her eyes.

"It's her home. Besides, she's the only one who can keep things running there."

"If she cared about us at all, she'd be here with us."

"I'm sure she will come if we need her." Nyx closed the gold pendant. "Maybe we should talk to Lyra. I mean the queen." It was hard to know what to call the woman who had served as a mentor to her. But she had to remember that wasn't Lyra. The queen was just using Lyra's body as a vessel.

"Why would we talk to her? I don't have anything to say." Niamh put her hands on her hips. "She tried to kill you. What makes you think she'd tell you the truth about anything?"

"She's the only one with answers, and mind whisperers can't lie to each other."

"Nyx?" a voice called out for her.

They turned as Novia blurred towards them.

Niamh furrowed her brow. *What's she doing here? Did you summon her?*

No, I didn't.

"Weren't you supposed to be on Glenfel?" Niamh asked. "Who's taking care of the prison?"

"The druidons. I'm so happy to see you both." Novia threw her arms around Nyx, then went to Niamh, who backed away.

Niamh!

What? I don't like being touched.

"How did you get through the shield?" Nyx asked.

"Your druid gave me a crystal." Novia fished a small opaque stone out of her pocket. "It's infused with power from Ambrose's staff."

"Why are you here?" Niamh crossed her arms. "You said you didn't want to come back with us when we returned from Glenfel."

"Nyx's druid called me. We've been talking about moving the queen to Glenfel. She'd be a lot more secure there." Novia brushed her curly green hair behind her ear. "Besides, I said I would join you once I was sure the prison was in good hands. We just need to figure out how to get her there securely." She glanced around. "What is this place?"

"Looks like the place Lyra stayed in when she tortured

those people — the ones she had Ambrose kill." Nyx hesitated. "We found this." She flipped open the gold locket. The image flared to life again.

Novia put a hand over her mouth as she gasped. "Is that…"

"Us." Niamh grimaced. "I still don't believe it."

"I suggest we find out." Nyx closed the locket. "Time to talk to our possible mother."

"This is a bad idea," Niamh stated for about the hundredth time as they approached the sealed well.

A month had passed since the former Queen of Andovia had attacked them and tried to kill Nyx. In defeating her, Nyx and her sisters had trapped the immortal queen at the bottom of the well when neither she nor the body she was possessing could escape from.

"Which is why I'll be the one talking to her." Nyx doubted either of her sisters would want to talk to the queen.

Niamh would get angry and Novia wouldn't want to face the woman who had imprisoned her.

Flames shimmered over the well that sealed the queen inside. Nyx and the others had been coming to check it every day to make sure the magic they had used to trap the queen stayed in place.

"But what if she tries to kill you again?" Niamh put her hands on her hips.

Novia bit her lip. "She's right. What if something goes wrong and we can't get to you?"

"If we all join powers, I can project myself down there." Nyx sat down by the well. "That way the queen can't get to me. Her powers shouldn't be able to get through the barrier."

"How do you know that won't give her a chance to

escape?" Niamh shook her head. "I don't like this. Let's call the druid."

"I agree. She's still dangerous." Novia knelt beside her.

"Darius can't hear us through the shield."

"He will probably still hear you since you are bound to each other." Niamh pulled out her knives as she crouched on Nyx's other side.

"We are linked, not bound. And it's a projection. She can't hurt me. So put your knives away." She didn't want to call Darius unless she had to. He wouldn't like the idea of her talking to the queen either.

Niamh scowled. "No. I'm going to be ready in case that witch tries anything."

Nyx took their hands and closed her eyes. Their powers merged. Light flashed around her as she reappeared in the hole as an astral projection. The well appeared wider than she'd expected. Shadows danced around the shafts of light. Lyra's body lay on the other side of the space.

The former queen lay there, unmoving. Her skin had paled and hollowed out. Only the queen's spirit would have kept that body alive. Her eyes remained closed.

Nyx hesitated and bit her lip. "Lyra?"

That got no response. Maybe she had fallen asleep.

"Lyra, wake up," Nyx raised her voice.

Still no response.

She sighed. "Or should I call you Mother?"

The queen's glowing eyes flew open. "You know." Her lips curled into a sneer.

"So it's true, then? But how can that be?" Nyx took a step back, uneasy under the queen's gaze. Mother or not, the queen had tried to kill her more than once already. She wouldn't trust her.

"Who else could be your mother? We are the last of our kind."

"But — but I don't understand. Your children were killed."

"Yes, they were. And don't call me Lyra. The time for pretences is over."

"Then how are me and my sisters here? Did you and Ambrose have more children after you… died? Is that how we're here?"

The queen snorted. "That would make you Lyra's children — which you aren't. You wouldn't be mind whisperers if you had her tainted blood."

"Then explain how this is possible." She crossed her arms. "Because I'm really trying hard to understand all of this."

Be more forceful, Niamh demanded.

Let her talk. Novia sighed.

Forget that. Demand answers.

The queen struggled into a sitting position. "If you want answers, get me out of this hole. Then I'll explain everything."

"That won't happen. And if you won't give me answers, then there's no reason for me to be here." Nyx closed her eyes.

"With my book, you could release your father from my enchantment."

"What book?" She narrowed her eyes as she opened them again.

"I have a book. A grimoire that contains all of my magical knowledge. All of the Twelve had one. If I help you save Ambrose then —"

"Then nothing. No one is going to free you. What kind of mother kills her own daughter? But I guess after you locked up Novia and sent Niamh to assassinate me, I shouldn't be surprised."

The queen snorted. "Isabella hired Niamh to kill you,

9

not me." The queen reached out to make a grab for her. Her hand passed straight through Nyx's form. "I need a blood link to restore me to my body. You, as the oldest of my triplets, are the strongest. If I can get back into my body, we could be a family —"

She clenched her fists. "We're not family. My sisters and I mean nothing to you. If we did, you would have told us the truth—"

"Would you have listened?" the queen scoffed. "You're as stubborn as I am."

"We'll do everything we can to make sure you never hurt anyone else." She closed her eyes and willed herself back to her body.

Nothing happened and the queen moved closer to her.

"I will get out of here. You can either side with me or against me. Consider that."

Nyx opened her eyes. "I'd never side with you."

"Would you rather the Archdruid continue to rule? He will destroy all of Erthea if he remains in power."

"No, but I doubt you'd be the one to bring about peace. Now let me out of here!" Nyx gasped as she opened her eyes and found herself back above the well with her sisters. She blew out a breath. "We need to get her to Glenfel. I don't think that will hold her for much longer."

CHAPTER 2

Darius Valeran stared at his former mentor's unmoving form propped up in bed. He chanted another spell. One for awakening. Magic pulsed through the air, but Ambrose didn't stir. He muttered a curse under his breath. What had the queen done to Ambrose? Why did she hate her husband so much?

He had almost run out of ideas of different things to try. Nothing over the last month had roused the other druid. He didn't have Ambrose's staff to experiment with either, since Nyx had taken it to go into the old city. Going to the Spirit Grove hadn't yielded any answers either. Nor had scouring through the spells in the Hall of Knowledge.

He paced up and down the length of the chamber with its bare grey stone walls. The only colour in the room came from the rich red velvet coverings on the fourposter bed. He ran a hand through his long wavy blonde hair. Weeks of research had done little good. There had to be a way to release Ambrose from whatever magic the queen had used on him.

He sighed. "Ambrose, if you can hear me, you need to tell me how to help you." He waited, but never got a response.

Nyx and her sisters hadn't had much luck getting through to him with their powers, either. Darius wondered how Ambrose had the strength to communicate with Nyx the way he had when the queen had tried to kill her. Why couldn't Ambrose do it again and tell them a way to fix him? Or maybe he had used the last of his strength to do that.

Darius flipped through the book further then his senses tingled.

Fergus Valeran stormed into the room. The Archdruid towered over him. His long dark blonde hair pulled back underneath his crown and his piercing blue eyes narrowed when he caught sight of his son.

"Father!" Darius shot to his feet.

"What's wrong with him?" The Archdruid motioned to the bed.

"He's...unwell."

Holy spirits, what was his father doing here? Fergus never came to visit him. His father had spent most of his life ignoring him. What had brought him here? Had Ambrose's absence been noticed? He thought he had done a good job making excuses as to why Ambrose was gone.

Fergus opened one of Ambrose's eyes. "He's not ill. He is in the grip of magic — which means that Andovian wench has somehow returned." His fists clenched. "Why have you been hiding this? Do you know where the queen is?" His eyes flashed with power, and the aura of energy around him increased.

No one in the world of Erthea was more powerful than the Archdruid, the highest authority over magickind. Energy crackled around his father like simmering flames.

"I found him like this. I didn't tell you because I wanted to find a way to save him." True enough. He knew he couldn't lie to his father and didn't dare to.

"Where's the queen?"

"I haven't seen her. Saving Ambrose has been my first priority."

Fergus paced. "How could she be back? I killed her. I wiped her miserable kind off the face of Erthea." He stopped pacing again. "You haven't told me why you never mentioned all this!"

Darius took a deep breath. He had to be careful. Anything could tip his father over the edge. "I was more concerned with helping Ambrose. How do you know she's back?" But he knew playing ignorance wouldn't last for very long.

"That's because he's been touched by a mind whisperer. He is under her control. Gods, I knew I should have killed him a century ago."

"But he hasn't proven to be a threat to you." Darius wouldn't let his father kill his mentor. Ambrose might not be perfect, but he'd been more of a father to Darius than Fergus had ever been.

Everyone knew Ambrose had once been the Queen of Andovia's husband. Some people said he'd been the one who helped the Archdruid take her realm and destroy her.

"Of course he's a threat. He is under her thrall." A fireball formed in Fergus' hand.

Darius stepped between Ambrose and the Archdruid. "Father, wait. If the queen is back, don't you think she would have used him by now? Keep him alive, use him." He had to say something to convince his father to keep Ambrose alive. Even if that meant Ambrose being imprisoned for a while. At least he would be alive.

Fergus hesitated, then snuffed out the fireball. "That's not a bad idea, boy. Are you sure you don't know where —"

"All I know is Lyra worked with Isabella. Isabella wanted to take your throne." That was true enough.

Fergus studied him for a moment. Most people wilted under the Archdruid's gaze, but Darius stood his ground.

13

"You'd better be telling the truth, boy. If you join with the queen against me, you will pray for death."

He laughed. "I'd never join her. You can believe that."

"Fine. Guards, take Ambrose away." Two of the Archdruid's personal guard came in and yanked Ambrose up by his arms. Ambrose's head lolled to one side and his long red hair spilled over his face.

"Where are you taking him?" Darius' heart pounded in his ears.

"Somewhere more secure. I won't have that Andovian imp using him as her puppet." Fergus chuckled. "Instead, I'll use him against her again. He always was her weakness." The Archdruid swept out of the room.

His older half-brother, Gideon, leaned against the doorframe and smirked. "What's the matter, brother? Scared your secrets will soon be discovered?" Gideon stood a head shorter than him. His long blonde hair darker than his own. They both had the same blue eyes as their father.

Darius' gaze hardened. "You're the one who told him about Ambrose." He should have known this was coming. Gideon might not have liked his mother very much, but he would have been incensed at her death.

Gideon's smile widened. "Of course I did. I know he helped condemn my mother. I know my mother was trying to find the Andovian witch. I'm guessing she found her."

"What does taking Ambrose away do? He's no threat to anyone."

"I need him to find the queen and that priestess who murdered my mother. If I have to use Father to do that, I will." Gideon glared at him. "You'd better decide whose side you're on. Be sure to not get in my way or I will put an end to you too." He then stormed off.

"My lord, the Archdruid commands you to come to the

palace at once." Another guard appeared in the doorway.

Wonderful. Had his father already woken Ambrose? Darius hadn't expected him to do that so fast. As much as he despised the palace, he knew he had to go.

Nyx? He reached out to her with his mind and hoped she'd hear him through the city's shield.

Yes? Anxiety came to him through their link.

Is the queen secure?

Yes, but…

But what? We found something. The queen is our mother.

Darius' eyes widened, but he didn't have time to ponder that. *You need to come to the palace. Make sure your sisters stay in the city. My father took Ambrose.*

Darius transported to the Crystal Palace in Alaris and found himself surrounded by an enormous crowd. He hadn't expected that. The palace stood like a glittering shush dual with its crystal walls and giant domed roof that glittered like a diamond.

Spirits, he hoped his father wasn't about to execute Ambrose. If Fergus viewed Ambrose as a true threat, he might kill him. But he hadn't expected this so soon. Fergus would need time to wake Ambrose and learn whatever he could from him.

Druid, Nyx called out to him as she pushed her way through the crowd.

"Stand aside," Darius commanded as the crowd parted. As the Archdruid's son he still had some authority.

Nyx hurried over to him. "Where is Ambrose?"

He noticed her usual pink plait had turned blonde and her wings appeared like a cloak. *Why are you glamoured?*

I figured it would be safer. I don't want to remind your father I am a mind whisperer now he knows about the queen. Nyx pushed her hair off her face.

"I don't know where Ambrose is. Gideon told my father about the queen."

"The Archdruid won't kill him — will he?"

"Where is he?" Novia asked as she and Niamh pushed their way over to them.

"I thought you two were —" Darius sighed.

"He's our father," Niamh hissed. "That means we have to save him. He might be the only way we have of getting our memories back."

"He —"

Trumpets sounded as the Archdruid and Darius' mother, Lady Mercury, stepped out onto the raised dais. Mercury stood next to his father, her long dark hair pulled back and wearing a triumphant look on her face. Her striking features twisted when she turned to look at Ambrose and her cool grey eyes narrowed.

"My people, I have dire news for you today." Fergus stepped forward. "The enemy we thought I'd vanquished a century ago has returned. The old Andovian Queen died, but my former wife and the head priestess from the great temple captured her soul and sought to use it against me." The crowd booed and shook their fists in anger. "I have someone who they thought they could use against me. Someone who claimed to be my ally."

The two guards dragged Ambrose out. The druid's head lolled to one side and his eyes remained closed.

Nyx caught hold of Darius's arm. *Don't do anything.*

His jaw tightened, and he shrugged her off. *I won't — even though I want to.* Trying to save Ambrose in front of all these people would only lead to more unwanted trouble. To save the other druid, he would have to find another way to get him away from his father.

"Isabella may be dead, but if Lyra Duncan thinks she and the queen can turn against me…" Fergus motioned with his hands. Glowing fiery light formed between his palms. "She's ensnared her own husband to use against me. Instead, I will use him to find her." He threw the whirling light at Ambrose. The magic hit the other druid and lit him up like a beacon as it blazed around him. Then the light shot into the sky and expanded in different directions.

"What's your father doing?" Niamh hissed.

"He is using Ambrose to trace the queen." Darius reached for Nyx's hand. To comfort her or himself, he didn't know.

They weren't supposed to show any kind of affection for each other in public. In that moment, he didn't care.

Will your father's magic get through the shield? Nyx squeezed his hand back.

Hopefully not, but we need to move the queen and soon, before my father finds her. Now my father knows she's alive he won't stop looking for her.

CHAPTER 3

Nyx wrapped her arms around Darius once they got back to his castle and clung to him for a moment. "I'm sorry. I know you wanted to save him. I did too. Gods, I never thought Gideon would turn your father against us."

Darius returned her embrace. "It was bound to happen sooner or later. We need to figure out a way to get the queen to Glenfel."

"Are you sure that's a good idea?" Novia took off her cloak. "The Archdruid's magic protects the island. What if his spell tracks her? We can't move her by boat now."

"How can we move her out of the city?" Niamh threw back her hood. "His spell will latch onto her the minute we get her through the shield."

Nyx pulled away from Darius and waved off her glamour. Her hair returned to its normal bright shade of pink and her purple wings unfurled. "Will the spell find her even if she's inside Lyra's body?"

"It might." Darius' face turned grim. "My father has nearly unlimited power at his disposal. We can't be sure the shield will be strong enough to withstand his attack."

Boom. The castle walls trembled.

Nyx gasped. "What was that?"

"My father's magic. It's here. I can sense it." Darius glanced around, uneasy.

"But why? The queen isn't here. Why would it come

here?"

Novia turned pale. "Oh gods, what if it's after me? Lyra — the queen, drained magic from me when she held me prisoner. Maybe she used it on Ambrose."

"Go into the old city. Now!" Nyx tossed Ambrose's staff to Niamh, then raised her hand. Both her sisters vanished in a swirl of green orbs.

"You should go with them." Darius touched her cheek. "Gideon told my father about Lyra. I can't be sure you'll be safe."

"No. Not without you." She shook her head. "You can come with me."

"You know I can't. My father is suspicious enough as it is, and I have to find a way to save Ambrose first."

Nyx crossed her arms. "We agreed to stay together no matter what."

She couldn't believe he would even suggest splitting up. Not after everything they'd been through. They were stronger when they were together, and she wouldn't go anywhere without him. She knew as well as he did what they destroyed was capable of and wouldn't leave him to face his father alone.

"Not at the expense of your safety." Darius put his hands on her shoulders. "Look, I don't want to be apart either, but I can't just disappear. I will follow you when I can, but first I have to try and get to Ambrose."

"Take a leave of absence. Make an excuse."

"We don't have much time. My mother will probably be here soon. She'll demand I go to the palace and then I can search for Ambrose —" he froze. "She's already here. Go!"

No. Nyx stood her ground. Her senses tingled as Mercury herself and several guards came in. Curse it. She hadn't expected them to come here so soon. Fumbling in her pocket, she slipped on a leather bracelet to hide their powers.

"Darius, your father's spell led us here." Mercury glanced between them and turned her attention to Nyx. "What a surprise. I always knew you were more powerful than —"

"Mother, the magic moved on." Darius stepped between her and Nyx. "Leave my servant out of this."

She hated being called a servant. She didn't serve him, but she knew they had to keep up appearances.

"Has she used her touch on you?" Mercury's dark eyes narrowed. "Gods above, I thought you would be safe from such power. I never should've let this monstrosity become your servant. I always knew she was dangerous."

"How could I? I'm not that powerful." She was glad she slipped on the bracelet that suppressed her powers. "Besides, I would never do anything to hurt him."

Mercury snorted. "We shall see." She raised her hand.

Nyx gasped as an invisible noose tightened around her throat. Somehow, Mercury could channel the Archdruid's power.

"Mother —"

Don't. Don't let her believe you're under my control. Nyx sank to her knees when Mercury let go of her.

"I don't sense the queen's spirit or much power in you. But looks can be deceiving. Guards, remove everything from her body." Mercury motioned at her.

"You will do no such thing." Darius shoved Nyx behind him. "And no, I'm not coming to the palace. So get out."

Nyx's eyes widened. *Wait, I thought you were going to go to the palace to save Ambrose?*

No, not if you are going to be at risk. Change of plan, we need to get out of here. If my parents treat you as a threat, you will be taken into custody as well. I can't allow that to happen.

"What did you say?" Mercury's mouth hung open.

"You heard me. I despise the palace. I'm not going. Now leave."

Mercury opened and closed her mouth several times before words came out again. "How dare you speak to me —"

Daris crossed his arms and scowled. "I do dare. I'm of age and as the Archdruid's son I outrank you. I will not be cooped up in the palace. I have duties here."

"But your safety —" Mercury protested.

"That's my problem, not yours."

His mother snorted. "You have no security here other than a few wards. You don't even have guards." She sneered at Nyx. "Or do you somehow think she is going to protect you?"

"I am in the Forest Guard and I can take care of myself. The queen isn't here and if she appears, I will deal with her."

"The Andovian Queen isn't just an enemy. She is immortal and —"

"And I'll deal with it," Darius repeated and gritted his teeth.

Don't we need to get Ambrose out? Nyx asked. *We need to be at the palace to do that.*

No, not now. Our priority is getting the queen out of Andovia. There's no way we could take Ambrose, not whilst he's in my father's custody.

"I won't leave you here with only that thing," — Mercury motioned towards Nyx — "and a house brownie for protection."

"Fine, I'll go to Trin and be with my siblings. That's remote and far safer than Andovia."

"Trin is a tiny island with only a few druids there."

"It's safe, and the island has its own protections. It's the perfect place to go." Darius took hold of his mother's arm and steered her towards the door. "You can leave now. Nyx, go and pack my things. Guards, get out."

The guards left and Nyx ducked around the corner but kept a close eye on Darius.

Mercury yanked her arm away. "I'm your mother. You can't treat me like this."

"You said you wanted me to be safe. On Trin I will be. Get out!"

"I taught you to behave better than this. Either you come to the palace or I'll have the guards drag you there."

"Why? So Father can use me as his next vessel?"

Nyx flinched, surprised. What had made him say that? It was better if they didn't reveal how much they knew about the Archdruid.

Mercury gasped. "Of course not. How could you know about that?"

"It doesn't matter. Just as long as you and Father stay away from me. I won't be used by him."

"Darius, I would never let him do that to you."

"Yes, you would. You would do anything to keep him in power."

"That's —"

"The truth. Now go!"

To Nyx's surprise, Mercury walked away.

"Why did you tell her —?" Nyx asked.

"Because it was the only way to make her leave. We need to go."

"To Trin?" She knew Trin was a small island occupied by the other druids, but it was on another continent, leagues from Andovia.

"No, somewhere safer. Now I have an excuse to leave, but we need to move fast. Go and pack your things. We need to get out of here. My mother will probably send more guards to get me."

Nyx headed to her room. She rarely slept in there. Most of the time she slept next to Darius. She shoved clothes, books and other items into her pack. It felt strange to be leaving this place after calling it home for the past few weeks. But it didn't matter where they had to go as long as she and Darius stayed together.

Outside, she found Darius and his dragon, Sirin. The large white dragon sat patiently waiting beside him. "Are you sure you've got everything? We need to take whatever we can with us."

"As sure as I can be. Are you sure we can stay in the old city? Most of it is in ruin."

"We'll manage."

"What about food and water? I doubt much grows there and we can't hunt for food there either." She swung her pack over her shoulder. Gods, she hadn't even considered that before. If they were going to be stuck there for a while, they would need food and other things to live on.

"Let me worry about that." Darius waved his hand and light blazed around his castle. "There. The castle's protections are activated, so it should keep anyone out whilst we're gone. Though I'm not sure we'll be coming back here anytime soon."

"We can't permanently stay in the old city, can we?" Nyx put her hand to her face. She only ever thought of the city as a place of refuge. Could it become a permanent home?

"Where are we going, boy?" Ada came out carrying a bag. The small woman with bark-like skin barely came up to their knees.

"You're coming with us?" Nyx arched an eyebrow.

"Of course I am. Someone needs to keep you two fed, don't they? Besides, from what I've heard about the city, it will need a lot of cleaning up."

They all scrambled onto the dragon. Darius placed Ada at the front of him, since she was the smallest. Nyx sat behind him as usual. As they took to the air and rose higher, dark shapes circled around them.

"Holy spirits," Darius gasped.

"What's that?" Nyx furrowed her brow. "Please tell me it's not what I think it is."

"The Dragon Guard. I can't believe she'd send them after me. Sirin, we need to hurry. If we don't get out of their range soon, they could knock us out of the sky."

Nyx muttered an oath under her breath. "Not just you. Your father's spell led them here when I sent my sisters there." Nyx traced glowing runes in the air. Each symbol sparked with light and energy crackled around them.

A glowing portal formed around them, and Sirin dove straight through it. They re-emerged a few seconds later, close to Varden Forest.

"Quick, open the shield before the Dragon Guard gets here," Darius urged her.

More shadows moved towards them in the distance. She raised the crystal that she had imbued with power from Ambrose's staff. The shield flared to life.

A dark cloud hovered over them. An enormous black dragon filled the sky and bore one rider.

The Archdruid.

Nyx gasped and gripped Darius tighter. *Come on, shield, open.*

More Dragon Guards appeared and swarmed around them like angry bees.

Below, the shield slowly opened.

The Archdruid's dragon advanced towards them and sent out a column of raging fire.

Sirin moved to dodge it, then screeched as the fire struck her underbelly. Nyx, Darius and Ada all screamed as they were thrown from the falling dragon.

Nyx raised her arms and released her magic to stop them all from plummeting to the ground. She flapped her wings hard to keep herself airborne. Sirin and Ada both became suspended in mid-air, but Darius continued to plummet.

"No!" Nyx cried out and dove towards him, her hand outstretched. "Druid, grab onto me!"

No, you need to get to safety. Go! Darius raised his hands and a blast of energy sent her hurtling away from him. The shield parted and dragged Nyx, Sirin and Ada through, then closed behind them.

"No!" Nyx scrambled to her feet after she hit the ground and pressed her hands against the shield. She couldn't believe what he had done.

Raising the crystal, she commanded the shield to open again, but this time it wouldn't budge.

"Open, damn you!" She pounded against the wall of energy, but no matter what she did, it refused to open.

The Archdruid's dragon caught hold of Darius between its powerful jaws, then turned and flew away with him.

A few moments later, the shield flashed as columns of fire rained down on them. Sirin flew over the trees until they reached the palace.

Nyx. Sirin crawled over to her, whimpering in pain. *He's gone.*

Tears stung her eyes, but she refused to let them fall. "Why did he do that? I could have grabbed him and pulled us both through."

"You can't blame him for wanting to keep you safe, deary." Ada came over and patted her back. "Come on, we need to get somewhere safe. That is what he would want us to do."

"I will get him back even if I have to take the shield apart," she snarled and gritted her teeth. She ran a hand through her hair and took several deep breaths. It did little to ease the whirling emotions inside of her.

Dragon fire blasted against the shield, exploding everything in its wake. How long would that shield stay up? Was it strong enough to withstand the constant onslaught of fire? Now he knew the queen was alive, the Archdruid wouldn't stop trying to come for her or Nyx and her sisters.

She'd hoped the old city would be a refuge, but now it felt more like a prison.

"What's to stop them from seeing us?" Ada asked. "They might be able to follow us."

"Ceilt doileir." Nyx waved her hand and chanted in the druid tongue. Mist blurred around the glowing shield. "Now they can't see us."

"This place is all ruin. Where are we going to stay?" Ada frowned.

"That's a good question." Nyx wondered if Darius had really thought this out. But then they hadn't had time to. It was either this or being forced to stay at the Crystal Palace. "We'll find somewhere. Let's go."

CHAPTER 4

Niamh winced as the sound of explosions shook the house she and Novia had been searching through. Her hands went to the knives sheathed at her waist.

"What's happening?" Novia came in and put a hand to her chest.

"Sounds like something is being fired."

After Nyx had sent them to the outskirts of the city, they hurried through the shield just as the Archdruid's spell had come after them. The magic had missed them by mere inches.

They hurried outside and flashes of light filled the sky.

"What's that?" Novia gasped.

"It's dragon fire." Nyx stumbled over to them, followed by a dragon and a small woman with shrivelled bark-like skin. "The Archdruid sent the Dragon Guard to attack the city."

"Are we safe?" Niamh didn't like the thought of being trapped inside the shield. "Can we leave?"

"Not for a while." Nyx grimaced. "The Archdruid will keep trying to bring the shield down. We have to stay here. It's not safe for us either."

"So we're all stuck here?" Niamh's mouth fell open. "How are we supposed to survive? We don't have food or water. Or shelter — most of the buildings were destroyed when your father took the city."

Novia furrowed her brow. "Where's the druid?"

Nyx looked away. "The Archdruid took him just as we were about to come through. The stupid fool gave himself up to protect us."

"I'm so sorry, Nyx." Novia put a hand on her shoulder.

"I will get him back. I'm not letting the Archdruid harm him." Nyx's hands clenched into fists.

"I think we need to focus more on helping ourselves right now," Niamh remarked. "How are we going to get food here? Or water?"

"It's easy enough to summon water, and there is a river not far from the palace. I can use magic to conjure food, too. I have a lot of experience during that and the prison," Novia replied. "Our first priority should be shelter. Then we need to work out how to get the queen to Glenfel."

Niamh snorted. "How? We'll never get out undetected. And we would need the druid there to help us."

"We'll figure something out. Getting into the palace would help. There are maps there and information about the city." Nyx put down her pack. "Maybe we should use the staff. Perhaps our combined magic will let us in."

"How do you know what's inside the palace?" Niamh frowned.

"The Archdruid taught Darius about the city and he shared his knowledge with me."

They all headed towards the palace. The dome-shaped building with sandstone walls loomed ahead of them.

Sirin stumbled along behind them, carrying Ada. Nyx spent some time applying a healing balm to the dragon's belly. She didn't know much about caring for dragons and hoped it would be enough to heal the beast.

"We've already tried getting in before," Niamh pointed out. "It didn't work. The queen probably locked the place up to make sure no one else can go inside."

"Yeah, but the three of us didn't try." Nyx moved to her side and took hold of Ambrose's staff from Novia. "If we're Ambrose's daughters, we should be able to wield its power."

Novia gripped the staff, too. "What are we supposed to do?"

"Try using the druidic language," Nyx said. "We need to focus our attention on what we want."

Niamh arched an eyebrow at her sister. "I don't know any druid words. I grew up with elves and assassins."

"I don't know it either." Novia shook her head.

"I know it. *Oscaite.*" Nyx raised the staff, and the crystal flared with light. "Open the door." Light shot from the staff and shimmered over the palace. With a loud groan, the enormous double doors swung open.

All three sisters peered into the gloom. Glowing yellow eyes stared back at them. They screamed as something hissed and slithered towards them.

Niamh let go of the staff and grabbed her knives.

The creature had the upper body of a woman and the lower body of a snake. It hissed at them again, but instead of attacking it headed straight for Sirin and Ada.

"No, stop!" Nyx held up the staff and pointed it at the creature. "We are the queen's daughters and you're not to harm any of us."

Niamh unsheathed her knives and prepared to throw them at the strange creature. *Good gods, what is that thing? There wasn't supposed to be anyone in the old city.*

The snake woman's eyes flashed, then she vanished in a whirl of light.

"That was…odd." Niamh lowered her knives. "How did you know she'd listen to you?"

"I didn't. I figured the queen or Ambrose set her up so she wouldn't kill us."

Niamh scoffed. "I doubt our dear mother cares about our safety."

"Let's look around and see how habitable this place is. I doubt the Archdruid would have had much time to destroy everything," Nyx remarked.

Novia nodded. "We should split up."

"Is that wise?" Ada clutched her bag to her chest. "This place doesn't look safe."

"It will take forever to check everything if we don't."

"I'll go and find the kitchens. See if there's anything usable in this place." Ada walked off.

"Shouldn't one of us go with her?" Nyx asked. "Sirin, go and keep an eye on her."

The dragon cocked her head to one side.

"This place is big enough for you. Go on." Nyx motioned after Ada.

Sirin huffed and strode off.

Niamh still found it odd having a dragon around. Unlike Nyx and Darius, she couldn't understand the creature very well.

She and Nyx headed off in one direction. Novia went off with the brownie and dragon.

"Are you sure that shield will hold up?" Niamh remarked.

"It's lasted a century."

"Yeah, but the Archdruid hasn't attacked it in years. Now he knows the queen is back. He won't stop attacking it until he gets through."

"It will hold. Maybe now we're here, we can find out what powers it."

"We won't be stuck here forever, will we?" Niamh hated being stuck in one place for too long. It made her uneasy.

"At least no assassins will come after you here." Nyx smiled.

"I can handle assassins. Do you remember this place?"

Nyx shook her head. "Not really. It feels familiar to me, but I can't remember ever being here."

"Me either. Maybe we can figure out why. At least I hope we can." Niamh opened the double doors that led to another hallway. "Too bad we can't use our powers on the queen. What is her name, anyway? I'm not calling her Mother."

Nyx shrugged. "No one seems to mention it. All the records call her the queen. Or we could call her by her title of Morrigan."

"She must have a name."

"Names have power. Maybe that's why we don't know it."

"I wonder if we have our real names. I knew the name Niamh, but nothing else when they found me."

"We've come full circle. We must have been here at some point. That locket showed us standing in front of the palace."

Niamh didn't want to believe the image they'd seen. Part of her wanted to go back to blissful ignorance. Maybe it had been better not knowing anything about their past. But she wouldn't give up her sisters for anything. If that meant having to deal with having the queen as her mother then so be it.

The doors led to another room. Filled with tables and chairs. Dust covered every inch of the furniture and of the floor.

"Everything here looks untouched." Niamh put a hand to her nose to stop herself from sneezing.

"They didn't have time to loot the palace since everyone was forced out when she died. With no one here, no one would take anything."

"Then why was the palace sealed up with that snake

woman standing guard? You said you sensed minds when we were here a few days ago. What if the city isn't uninhabited like we thought?" Loud thumps echoed above them. "How long will they keep up the attack on the shield?"

Nyx shrugged. "They won't give up easily. They'll keep going until the shield comes down. Or at least keep trying to bring it down."

"It will take forever to search these rooms. You take one side; I'll take the other." She flung open another door and froze when Master Oswald stood before her.

Niamh couldn't believe it. How could a leader from the Order of Blood have followed her here? She knew the other assassins would come after her, but how could he have got through the shield? This place was off-limits to anyone but her and her sisters who had a way of getting in and out of the old city.

Could it be him? It had to be. There was no mistaking his weathered face, his long white hair, or piercing blue eyes. She would know the face of the man who had raised her anywhere.

"Traitor!" He advanced towards her with a sword raised, magic flared in his free hand.

"No, you can't be here." Niamh grabbed her knives.

"What are you doing?" Nyx rushed down the hall to her.

The form of Oswald shifted into a man with grey hair and piercing dark eyes.

"Holy spirits." Nyx gasped.

"Told you, you belong to me, Nyxie. You'll never escape me." The man, who had resembled Master Oswald before, sneered at her.

All colour drained from her face and she backed away.

Niamh slammed the door shut. "Don't go to that room."

"But — but how did he come back? He's gone — I banished him."

"It must be a demon or some kind of shapeshifter. Master Oswald can't be here and I didn't sense his energy."

"That wasn't Harland?"

Harland, the man who had raised Nyx. It took a moment to place the name.

"No. Let's keep looking. I hope there's no more monsters lurking around this place."

CHAPTER 5

Novia wondered if she'd gone mad when she decided to return to Andovia. She knew this place held nothing but danger. At least on Glenfel, she had some semblance of safety. Worse still, she'd had to leave her friends and the people in the Underlight behind.

She couldn't ignore the need to be with her sisters. As triplets, they were part of each other. Besides, they'd never figure out their missing past unless they stuck together. She only intended to take a short leave of absence from the island. The druidon guards might keep the prison in order, but they still needed a warden.

Too bad she wouldn't be leaving the old city any time soon. How long would they be stuck here? Weeks? Months? Indefinitely?

Novia had hoped to convince her sisters to return to Glenfel with her. They would be safer there. But Nyx would never leave Darius. That much she knew. Having her owl Archie around would have made her feel better. Gods, Archie. He wouldn't be able to reach her now. She'd told him to call her if anything went wrong on Glenfel.

The palace proved to be a winding maze of corridors. She hated being trapped inside. It reminded her of that small chamber the queen had kept her locked up in after she had kidnapped her and brought her back to the old city.

There had to be a way to navigate the palace. She drew magic and blurred through the different rooms. No buzz of minds came to her. She hoped there weren't any more creatures lurking within the palace walls.

Pushing open another door, crystal torches on the wall flared to life. Three beds stood on one side of the chamber. Something with glowing crystal animals hung from the ceiling, with three dragons on it. Had this been their bedchamber when they were children?

The queen was their mother. Bile rose in her throat at the thought of that. Weren't mothers supposed to be kind and loving? Ophelia, the woman who'd raised her, had been strong but fair. Someone who'd accepted her and taught her as best she could.

The queen had kidnapped her and held her prisoner in the old city for days and drained Novia's energy. That awful chamber haunted her dreams every night. It was why she never wanted to set foot in the old city again.

Light blurred around Novia. Her head spun until she found herself in a darkened room. "Oh gods," she gasped.

Why had her power taken her from the palace to the temple where the queen had locked her up? Did her power want to torment her now?

Shadows danced along the grey stone walls as the wind stirred up the dirt and deadened leaves on the flagstone floor.

Running to the door, her heart pounded, and she gasped for breath. *I can't be here. I won't stay here...*

She found herself back in the temple. Not long after she'd been taken...

"Where am I? Why did you bring me here?" Novia sat huddled in the corner with her knees pulled up to her chest.

Something moved in the corner of the room and dragged her out of her memory.

Novia's hand went to the knife at her belt. "Who's there?"

Glowing amber eyes stared back at her.

She backed away, pulling out her dagger and conjuring orbs of green light. The light chased away the shadows, revealing a large grey skinned dragon. One of the Dragon Guards mounts no doubt. How had it got in here? Most of the dragons they had found so far had been outside of the city, not in the centre of it.

Should she talk to it? Tell it to go away?

Her heart pounded faster, and she froze as her mind wandered back to her imprisonment again. *The queen grabbed her by the throat and lifted her off her feet.*

"Your power is hardly worth taking, but I need my strength back…"

The dragon came closer and nudged her with its head.

Novia wrapped her arms around it and tears dripped down her face. Under normal circumstances, she knew such a thing would be complete madness.

You're safe. She can't harm you anymore. The dragon's voice washed over her like a welcoming embrace. *The queen is gone and I won't let her hurt you again.* The dragon flipped her onto its back and carried her out.

Novia wiped her tears away and took several deep breaths. She had to calm down. To regain her composure. Her sisters had both encouraged her to talk about what happened, but she didn't want to. Instead, she just wanted it all to go away and pretend like it had never happened.

What was wrong with her? She didn't have time to act like a child. Her sisters needed her.

"I can… I can understand you." She rubbed her eyes again. "But how? My power doesn't work on dragons." She hadn't had much luck talking to Sirin.

I'm not a dragon — I'm a spirit animal — an animas.

"A what?"

I'm yours and you're mine. I'm glad to have found you again.

"Again? What do you mean?" She furrowed her brow. "Have we met?"

We were together before.

I will show you. The dragon took off.

Novia gasped, then laughed as the wind rushed against her. This was true freedom. Not being stuck in that awful temple allowed her to breathe easy again.

The palace loomed ahead. To her surprise, the dragon didn't land like she expected. Light flared around them.

She yelped as their bodies transformed into energy and passed straight back into the bedchamber she'd been in earlier.

We were here before. A long time ago, when you were a child.

"Here? You were mine… Before I…died?" She couldn't be sure she and her sisters had been dead, but something happened to them. Something that erased their memories. "What's your name?"

They called me Five in the Guard.

"I meant your real name."

The dragon shook its head. *I don't remember.*

Her heart sank. "Something erased your memories too. Curse it!" Her hands balled into fists. "Well, you need a new name. I'll call you Andre. Now I need to find my sisters." She furrowed her brow as she spotted glowing lights moving across a black wall of crystal.

One green. One gold. Nyx and Novia. It had to be them as she sensed their presences.

Maybe she had found a missing piece of the past after all.

"Come, Andre. My sisters will be so excited to see meet you. I can't wait for them to find their spirit animals as well. Are you —?" Novia stopped when she realised the dragon had vanished.

Where had Andre gone, and why had he vanished?

CHAPTER 6

It seemed to take forever to find her way back to Novia. Nyx found her on the first floor. Niamh was still exploring on the ground floor. They could call each other in full if they needed to. And Niamh insisted she'd be fine.

"Nyx, look what I found. It shows where we are on the screen." Novia motioned to a glowing panel on the wall. "It's incredible. This magic must be a crystal technology we've never seen before. There's us." She motioned to the three glowing dots.

"That must be Niamh." She pointed to the glowing dot below them. "And Ada. Is anyone else around?" After seeing that creature that changed into Harland, she dreaded to think what else they might find lurking around the palace.

"Why would there be?" Novia furrowed her brow.

"Because Niamh and I have already found a couple of different creatures in rooms on the ground floor. This place isn't as empty as we thought." She glanced at the screen again. "Did you find anything else?"

Novia bit her lip. "Maybe. I saw one of the dragons — well, it's not really a dragon. It's a kind of shapeshifting spirit animal that looked like a dragon. But he vanished before I could ask him any more questions."

"A shapeshifting what?" Nyx's frown deepened. "We need to be careful. I doubt anything we find in this palace could be considered good. There's no telling how dangerous the other magickind here are."

"I didn't find him here. I found him outside of the palace."

"When did you have time to go out of the palace?"

Novia waved a hand in dismissal. "A few minutes ago. I found him inside the old temple. He brought me back to the palace, but then he vanished." She blew out a breath. "We had shape shifting spirit animals when we were children — that's what he told me."

"And you believed him?"

"I don't see any reason why he would lie. I didn't sense any deception from him."

One good thing about being mind whisperers was their power allowed them to see the truth no matter how hard people tried to hide it from them.

She didn't doubt Novia's judgement — her sister was no fool — but they all had to be on their guard.

"Don't be so quick to trust anyone. We have no idea what we might be up against here."

"But I thought everyone was forced out after the queen died?" Novia turned away from the glowing screen. "You said even the Andovians were forced out."

"Maybe not all of them were. We know Ambrose remained when he hid the queen's body." Nyx grimaced. "So a few people must have stayed behind – like those the queen had Ambrose kill when she was searching for her corpse." Nyx put her hands on her hips. "Too bad there's not someone alive who could show us where —"

Light flashed as a glowing form of a woman appeared. Nyx yelped and light shot from her hand. The light burst through the glowing woman and evaporated against the wall.

The woman stared at them as if she expected something.

Odd, Nyx half expected the woman to berate her for hitting her with magic.

The woman's long raven hair fell past her shoulders, pointed ears picked out through it, and her violet eyes roamed over them. Her long white gown shimmered along with the rest of her body.

Nyx and Novia glanced at each other.

Talk to her. That snake woman responded to you, Novia remarked.

Why me?

Because you're the oldest and I don't want to talk to her.

She rolled her eyes. "Who… Or what are you?"

"I'm the palace keeper. How may I serve you?"

"Serve us? What are you?" Nyx didn't know whether to be fascinated or alarmed by the woman.

"The keeper — you watch over and protect the palace, don't you?" Novia asked. *See, she's like the keeper that we've seen in the Hall of Knowledge. That means she probably won't hurt us.*

The woman nodded. "I serve those in need."

"Why were you responding to my sister's voice?" Novia wanted to know.

"You are the Morrigan's heirs."

The Morrigan. Their mother. Maybe they should call her that since mother would never sound right.

Nyx furrowed her brow. "Keeper, can you tell us why there are creatures roaming around the palace? Who are they?"

"Oh, you mean the prisoners."

"What prisoners?" Her frown deepened. *Gods, do you think the queen still kept prisoners in the city?*

Novia flinched. "That makes sense. The prisoners were probably somewhere warded. Some must've got out. How many prisoners were kept by the queen?"

"Over one hundred on record, but the queen had many more. She had many enemies."

No surprise there.

"Get us a list of prisoners with their names, powers, and crimes," Nyx said. "Does anyone else live here?"

"A few prisoners. But most of them live outside of the palace in the forest now — they are too afraid of the queen returning to stay here."

She ran a hand through her hair and sighed. "Wonderful. There could be dozens of people living here. I doubt they will be very welcoming towards us." Niamh appeared in a flash of light. "How did you do that?"

"I touched the screen when I saw glowing dots. I guessed it must be you two. Nice. We can transport from place to place like you do."

"We need to be careful. There are prisoners running loose." Novia grimaced. "This place isn't as safe as we thought."

"Prisoners? How are they still alive?"

"Maybe all the stories Darius heard are true. There were legends about Andovia being the home to the ancients — the first magickind. And they held a wealth of knowledge and power," Nyx said. "Including the ability to produce limitless food so its people would never go hungry. It's one of the reasons why the Archdruid wanted this realm so much."

"Do we need to round up the prisoners?" Niamh's hands went to her daggers. "If people are going to start attacking us, I say we should attack them first. We have enough problems without dealing with them."

"We don't know how many there are. There's not enough of us to round up dozens of magickind." Novia shook her head. "The best way to contain them would be to lead them all to an area where we could trap them."

"Keeper, can you get the prisoners out of the palace?" Nyx asked.

They needed somewhere safe to stay, not somewhere overrun with enemies. Since this had been their home when they were children and still had wards in place, it would be the safest place for them to stay.

"Of course." Light flared over the screen.

"Can you ward the palace so nothing else can come in?" Nyx persisted.

"The wards are raised. No one, not even spirits, can enter now."

She breathed a sigh of relief.

They all headed up to the next floor, where they found dozens of bedrooms and more of those odd screens. Nyx found the strange magic that operated them fascinating. Niamh wandered off to explore by herself again.

"Maybe we shouldn't stay here," Novia mused as they searched through the different rooms.

"Where else can we go?" Nyx opened another door. All the bedrooms looked immaculate. Most as if they had been left untouched over the last century.

Dust covered everything in a white layer, but everything seemed to be intact. Oddly, she expected them to be ransacked, or at least destroyed, if people were still living within the boundary of the old city.

"I don't know. Perhaps Glenfel. It would be safer there than trapped inside a shield that could come down at any moment."

"With the Archdruid back in the realm, I doubt Glenfel will be safe, either. What's stopping him from going there? It's his prison, remember?"

"I'd rather the queen was there than here, where she has power. I know Glenfel better than anyone, and I could keep an eye on her there."

"You're not going to stay here with us, then?" She didn't like the idea of her sister leaving again. They were stronger if they all stayed together.

"You can talk about what happened to you," Nyx added.

Novia narrowed her eyes. "There's nothing to talk about."

"Still, I'm here for you if you need me." She squeezed her sister's shoulder.

"You perhaps, but not Niamh. She doesn't like messy emotions."

"That doesn't mean she's heartless. Either of us could be like her if we ended up in Ereden."

Novia didn't look convinced. "She hates me."

"No, she doesn't."

"How do you know that?"

"Because we don't know what's in her heart. We have to stick together. We're stronger that way." Nyx pushed her hair off her face. "Now I need to figure out a way to save my druid and Ambrose."

She still couldn't believe Darius had let himself be captured like that. Part of her wanted to break down and cry. She wouldn't. She had to stay strong for her sisters.

"How? He told you not to go after him." Novia opened the door and peered into another room. "Wouldn't he want you to stay as far away from Crystal Palace as possible?"

"I'm not leaving him behind. You have no idea what his father will do to him. I do. Besides, we can't let the Archdruid learn about you and Niamh or about where the queen is."

"He probably already knows she's here." Novia winced as the walls trembled.

Nyx searched Darius' knowledge. Most of what he knew about the city and the palace were rumours and stories. He hadn't been in the palace or seen it with his own eyes. That library and records room had to be around here somewhere.

"Keeper?" Nyx called out.

The woman appeared in a flash of light. "Yes, my lady?"

"I'm not a lady. I'm… Just me." Nyx tossed her plait over her shoulder. "Can you show me where the library is and how to get there?"

"I can't. Only the queen can access the library and Hall of Records. She sealed them off during the siege of the city."

"Okay. But where is it located?"

"I don't know. The location was erased from my knowledge."

Nyx sighed. "Never mind."

"Nyx, you should see this."

She turned to see where Novia stood. "What?"

"Look in here. I found this place earlier."

She went over to join her sister. The lights came on as crystal torches illuminated the walls.

It revealed a large chamber with murals of different animals. Chandeliers sparkled on the ceiling and all three beds lined one side of the room.

"It feels familiar somehow."

"I still can't believe we lived here."

"I doubt it was as wonderful as it sounds given who our parents are." Nyx went over to the bed on the left. "It's strange. I can't imagine living in a place like this."

This place was a world away from where she had grown up with her human tribe. Her life stealing on the streets of Joriam felt like a lifetime ago, rather than around eighteen months ago.

She ran a hand over the bed. Nothing came to her other than the feeling of familiarity.

Novia opened the drawers and cupboards, but they were

empty. "What happened to everything?"

She shook her head. "We lost a lot. I don't think we'll find answers in here."

CHAPTER 7

The two Dragon Guards dragged Darius to the Crystal Palace. At least Nyx and Sirin had escaped. Now he prayed she wouldn't come after him. It would be safer if she stayed in the old city with her sisters.

They pulled him into the great hall. Darius could have used his powers against them, but he really needed to find Ambrose. The guards dragged him across the sparkling oak floor. Overhead, crystal chandeliers glittered like diamonds.

Fergus rose from his throne. "Where's the mind whisperer?" He narrowed his eyes at the guards.

"She escaped." Mercury came in behind them and glanced at her son. "He helped her to get away with his dragon. The boy's clearly under her control."

Darius yanked his arms free from the guards' grip. "I'm not under anyone's control. She's not that powerful — you tested her yourself."

Gideon stepped out from behind the throne. "You could have shielded her power. I felt glimpses of it when I tested her."

"This is ridiculous."

"Why did you help her escape?" Fergus crossed his arms. "If the mind whisperer is as innocent as you say, then why not bring her before me?"

"Because I know what you'd do to her." Darius glared at his father. "This is all pointless."

"We know you're under her control. You've been seen together more than once." Mercury's lip curled in disgust. "No doubt you believe yourself in love with her because of her power. She sleeps in your bed, for goodness' sake!"

Darius winced. Damn, he thought, they'd been careful about keeping their relationship discreet. He thought they were safe at his castle, but no doubt his mother had spies everywhere. Who could have spied on them? Ada? She was the only other person who lived with them, but Darius didn't think she would betray them. Their friends Ranelle and Lucien stayed sometimes, but he doubted either of them would say anything. It didn't matter who had given them away.

"See, he doesn't even deny it." Mercury sneered. "Fergus, you must release him from her control. I will not have that witch use our son against us."

"Indeed." Power flared between Fergus' fingers.

"Wait, I thought a mind whisperer had to die for someone's soul to be released from their control?" Gideon held up a hand to stop their father.

"Usually, yes, but I can break a link between a mind whisperer and her victim. I've done it before." Fergus gave an evil smirk and lightning shot from his hand.

Darius cried out as lightning surged through him. Lightning was his element. It shouldn't hurt him. Yet pain flared through every nerve ending. The power burned through his shirt and the tattoos covering his torso flared to life.

All of a sudden, Fergus stopped, and the pain receded. The Archdruid stomped over to him. "What magic is this?"

Heat flared over his skin and glowing white runes appeared. They weren't like the sigils and druid runes his parents had carved into his flesh during their brutal training of teaching magic.

Fergus ran his fingers over one rune and drew back as static jolted him. "These are ancient fae marks. I haven't seen them in a lifetime. Where did you get them, boy?"

Darius glanced down at the marks. He hadn't known they were there.

Nyx. She must have etched them on him. They looked like the kind of symbols she sometimes used.

"I don't know. What are they?"

Mercury slapped him. "Only the Andovian Queen could have put these on you. You've been harbouring our enemy all this time."

That sounded so ridiculous. He laughed. "Nyx isn't the queen."

"These are protection runes. I can't break your bond with her," Fergus growled.

The doors opened, and the guard rushed him. The man felt one knee and bowed his head. "My lord, we tracked the mind whisperer to the old city. She somehow got through the shield."

Nyx was safe. For now, at least. He sighed with relief.

"And you say she's not the queen?" Mercury scoffed. "How else could she get through? Only the queen could pass in and out of the shield. Gods, we never should have let that girl roam free for so long. She has caused so much damage."

"Just get into his mind and find out what he knows. You're the Archdruid. No one is more powerful than you," Gideon snapped. "Maybe you can find a way into the city. That girl needs to die."

It looked like his brother and his parents were finally united in something. There would be no reasoning with them.

"I can't enter his mind with those runes on him." Fergus paced back and forth. "He is protected by ancient magic that is difficult to undo." His father grabbed his arm and slapped a metallic cuff onto Darius' wrist.

Oh no. He recognised it as a device that drained magic.

Mercury's hands curled into fists. "We will find another way. Once we release him from her power, he should return to normal. Gods, how could we have been so blind to not realise he was under her control?"

Darius wasn't about to let them do anything to him. He had to find Ambrose, then get to the safety of the old city. If his father's power couldn't hurt him, then maybe other things couldn't either.

He raised his hands and hit both guards with his lightning. Both men slumped to the ground. Darius turned and ran straight for the double doors.

"Stop!" Mercury cried.

The doors slammed shut. His father's magic, no doubt.

Darius gritted his teeth. He couldn't call Sirin to come help him here, either. He was on his own.

More guards, along with his parents, advanced towards him.

He needed something to distract them with. But what?

His mind raced with possibilities. Druid magic wouldn't help much — not against his father. Using sorcery and summoning spirits wouldn't do much good against his mother, either. Different came to his mind — something he picked up from Nyx.

"Avock!" He winced as light and energy exploded around the room.

Darius grinned and yanked the door open. He traced runes on the door to seal it. Then added a couple more that came to mind. Hurrying down the hall, he found an oncoming troupe of guards. He cast his senses out to detect Ambrose. Nothing came to him.

There would no time to search either. For he knew

Ambrose might not be in the palace.

Rounding another corner, he grabbed a guard by the throat. "Where's Ambrose Brethian?"

The guard struggled. "Upstairs, second floor. Under guard."

"Good." Darius punched him and knocked the guard unconscious.

He traced more runes and reappeared on the floor above. No one stood guard outside the door. He hesitated, but then sensed no one inside. Except Ambrose.

Why weren't there any guards? Fergus wouldn't leave any prisoner unattended.

Flinging open the door, he found Ambrose lying on a bed. Beside him stood a dark-haired woman. She had been biting Ambrose's wrist. Her eyes blazed with light and fangs protruded from her mouth. Long hair fell over her face, her skin appeared so pale it was almost translucent.

"What are you doing to him?"

She lunged for Darius. He raised his hand and fired a bolt of lightning at her. The woman dodged him and smiled. "You'll never take him."

The runes etched over his chest shimmered with white light.

The woman hissed and backed away.

Somehow, the runes must protect him from a lot more than his father's magic. He lunged towards the bed.

"Ambrose?" He shook his mentor. "Ambrose, wake up." The other druid's eyes remained glassed over. "Ambrose!" Darius gave him a jolt of energy, but he still didn't stir.

"You'll never wake him." The woman smirked. "He's lost."

He glared at her. "What have you done to him? What are you?"

She only laughed again.

His senses prickled; warning of more guards headed his way. Mercury and Fergus wouldn't be far behind. Rushing for the window, he blasted through it. Glass rained onto the ground below. He jumped and used magic to slow his descent, landing with a thud. Then he ran.

Darius knew he had to keep his magic usage to a minimum. Or else it would be a beacon for his parents to follow. He didn't stop running until he reached the stables. Horses were quick, but he needed something faster. No horse could outrun the Dragon Guard.

Ducking around the corner, he stopped and tapped the runes on his arms. Light flared around him as he activated a glamour spell. A linen tunic formed over his bare flesh. At least he could blend in a little more.

After bypassing the stables, he headed straight for the dragon enclosure. All beasts from the Dragon Guard were housed here. Giant, black scaled beasts were chained and caged. He hated seeing so much suffering. This would have been Sirin's fate if she had been born big and black.

An affinity for dragons had always been part of his gift. He could communicate and control them. The Dragon Guard used nothing but brute force and torture until they broke the dragons down.

Darius scanned each beast with his mind and winced. The dragons' suffering washed over him like a heavy cloud. Their spirits were broken. Most didn't care anymore. They did as commanded and didn't fight their captors.

One dragon thrashed and pounded at the bars of his cage. Its energy felt young, male, and strong. The perfect specimen for the Guard to break.

Stop now before you hurt yourself. Darius touched the dragon's mind with his senses.

The beast stopped thrashing and huffed. Its amber eyes

flashed. *You can speak…to me?*

Young, indeed. It hadn't learnt to communicate well.

I'm going to get you out of here, but you need to do something for me in return.

The dragon huffed. *I won't help you, sorcerer.*

I'm not a sorcerer. Well, not completely. I'm a druid. If you let me ride you and help me escape, I will let you go.

Why would I help you?

Isn't that better than being stuck here? Sooner or later, they will break you. Darius gripped the bars. *I can get you — all of you out of here.*

The other dragons didn't respond. He couldn't be sure they'd even heard him.

Get me out!

Do you have a name? He fumbled with the door.

They call me Four.

I'll give you a new one. Ember.

Dragons were a proud race and considered their names part of their souls.

Ember, the dragon repeated. *Get me out of here, druid.*

I'm Darius. He yanked the door open to one of the cages, then the others.

None of the other dragons moved.

Ember leapt out and stayed close to him.

Come on, you're free. Darius motioned for them to go.

None of them moved.

Leave them. They've been broken, Ember huffed. *Nothing you say will make them respond.*

They couldn't leave. If he did, the guards would use these creatures to chase him.

How could he get through to broken souls? He didn't have time to linger here.

Darius closed his eyes and concentrated on the feelings of flight, freedom, and independence. When he looked

53

again, some of them turned their heads in his direction. *You're not broken,* he told them. *You have a chance to run free. As you were born to be. Prove to them you're stronger than they are.*

Still, the others didn't move.

Come. Darius gave the mental command. *You will never answer to the Dragon Guard again. You will be free.* He scrambled onto Ember's back.

They don't know how to survive without commands, Ember remarked.

Maybe once we're safe, we can change that. Let's go.

One by one, the dragons stood and took to the air. Ember took the lead. Darius blasted the buildings with lightning so more dragons could get free.

Come, all of you. We're headed to the old city.

Darius! His friend Ranelle's voice rang through his mind.

Rae? What is it?

The Dragon Guard are here to arrest me. What's going on?

Spirits, he hadn't expected them to go after his friend so quickly. *Can you get out of the library?*

Yes, but where can I go? To your castle?

No, it's not safe there. The Dragon Guard is hunting me, too. Just be ready and I'll come to get you.

The swarm of dragons flew over Alaris like a dark cloud.

Rae, where are you? Darius glanced around the roof of the great library. The massive roof glimmered like copper in the noon sunlight.

Ranelle waved to him. Her fiery red hair blew around her face, and her green eyes were etched with concern. She wore a long green dress and held a large pack underneath her dark cloak.

Lucien appeared beside her. His mop of dark hair stood in a tangled mess, his dark eyes scanned his surroundings. He wore only a loose grey tunic, black trousers, and boots. It didn't look like he had had time to grab any belongings like Ranelle had.

Hurry, the Dragon Guard are here to arrest us, Lucien called.

Go, help my friends, he commanded to another young dragon. *Luc, Rey, climb on. And hurry.*

They did as he said.

Now to the old city.

Guards appeared below them and fired blasts of energy from their staff weapons. Blasts of gold light zipped through the air, hitting the surrounding building with loud booms.

Fire back! Darius motioned to the dragons.

Ember and the other dragons roared. Each dragon sent columns of fire, blasting the armoured guards off their feet.

The guards wouldn't die, but he hoped it would slow them down for a while.

Darius took the lead.

"What's going on?" Ranelle and Lucien flew alongside him. "What happened?"

"My father thinks Nyx is the Andovian Queen. Nyx and her sisters are safe. But the old city is under attack." Darius filled them in.

"Then why are we headed to the old city?" Lucien frowned.

"Because it's the only place we can go to escape my father. My parents think I'm under Nyx's control. There's no going back now." Darius knew his old life was gone. He'd never go back to working in the Forest Guard.

Now he didn't know what the future held. All that mattered was getting to Nyx and to safety.

CHAPTER 8

Nyx doubled over as pain tore through every nerve ending. She grabbed onto a tree for support.

"What's wrong?" Novia touched her shoulder.

"Gods." She clutched her chest. She'd never felt pain like this before and knew something had to be very wrong.

"Niamh!" Novia yelled. "Hurry, something's wrong with Nyx."

Niamh jumped down from a tree branch. "What?"

"Do something. She's in pain." Novia motioned to her.

Nyx shook her head. "It — it's not me. It's Darius. I can feel his pain." She sank to her knees. "Something is hurting him. I have to go."

"You can't —"

Nyx ignored them and vanished in the swirl of green orbs. She reappeared close to the shield near the old guard tower. Blasts of dragon fire pelted the shield and exploded around them.

Sirin came up beside her and rose on her hind legs. *Darius. He can't get through.*

Nyx gasped when she walked into the shield and a wall of energy flashed into existence. Overhead, more dragons swarmed like an angry cloud. One of the dragons hit a Dragon Guard with a plume of fire. The black beast bore a rider.

Her heart leapt.

Darius.

Ambrose's staff appeared in a flash of orbs. She raised it to open the shield. The glowing bubble of white light flashed but didn't open.

"Open!" She hit the shield with a burst of light from the staff. The magic bounced back at her. Nyx ducked, and the power exploded a tree behind her.

Darius' dragon shot out more bursts of fire at the other dragons. Several guards plummeted to the ground. Instead of finishing off the other dragons, they turned and fired at the guards, too. Darius' doing, no doubt.

Sirin thrashed against the shield. *Why can't I get through? I need to get to him.*

"I don't know. Maybe it's some sort of protection. Perhaps it won't allow anyone through when it's repelling magic." Nyx pressed herself against the shield.

One of the Dragon Guard's and his beast fired back. The blast struck Darius' dragon, causing it to howl in pain.

"Let. Me. Through." Nyx struck the shield with the staff. The wall of energy trembled but didn't open. "Sirin, take us higher." She scrambled onto Sirin's back. The dragon roared and rose above the trees.

The shield had to have a weakness somewhere. A part she could open. More blasts of energy batted against the glowing will of energy. The sound deafening as fire exploded around them.

Druid? Nyx reached out to him with her mind. Usually, the shield didn't let any magic pass through. Even speech in thought.

Nyx, you need to open the shield.

It won't open. Believe me, I'm trying. Make the dragons stop attacking. I don't think the shield will open when it's under fire.

Sirin beat her wings hard, then hovered as they reached the top of the shield.

"Stop!" Nyx reached up and energy flared against her fingers. The shield didn't budge when she raised the glowing staff again.

Nyx, what are you doing? Niamh called out to her.

She glanced down and spotted her sisters. *Trying to get the shield to open.*

Darius and his new dragon continued dodging and firing at the guards.

Druid, you need to use your power and make all the dragons stop. Using the staff against the shield still proved useless.

I've never used my power on that many dragons. I doubt it will work.

It only needs to be for a few moments.

"Sirin, get us to the ground again. I have an idea." Sirin huffed and headed back to the ground. "We need to use our powers to open the shield." She leapt from the dragon's back. She raised the staff and her sisters gripped it. The staff flared with their power. *Now, druid!*

Overhead, each dragon stopped and hovered in a daze.

Open, Nyx commanded. *Come through.*

Light blazed from the staff. The light expanded through the shield and dragged all of the dragons through. One by one, each of the dragons fell to the ground like stones.

"That wasn't supposed to happen." Nyx lowered the wooden staff.

Two dragons lay near them. One black and one larger red one.

Nyx hurried over to the black one. "Where's Darius?"

The dragon craned its neck towards her, curious.

Sirin flew over to her and snarled. *Where's my rider?*

He fell.

"Where?" Nyx demanded.

You can hear me. The black dragon blinked. *Are you like the druid?*

She's kindred, Sirin snapped. *Like my druid. If you try to harm her, I will tear you apart.*

Nyx's eyes widened. Sirin never acted aggressive to anyone. Most of the time, she was docile.

The black dragon bowed its head to her. A sign of respect among dragons.

"He must be here somewhere." She glanced around.

Novia came over. "Nyx, what are we going to do with all these dragons?"

"I have no idea. All I care about is finding Darius. Sirin, get in the air and look for him. He might be hurt. You go, too." She motioned to the black dragon.

To her surprise, both dragons flew off. If the other dragon caused any trouble, she knew Sirin would keep him in line.

"It's incredible how you talk to them," Novia breathed.

"I can talk to them through my link to Darius. But he always says anyone can talk to dragons if you learn how to listen."

"Sisters, this thing isn't moving," Niamh called over to them and motioned to the other fallen beast.

They came over and joined her.

"Maybe it got injured during the fall." Novia reached out to touch it.

Niamh slapped her hand away. "This is a dragon. Not a pet."

"She's right, Nov. Most of the Dragon Guards' beasts are mindless killers. Leave it. If it becomes a problem —"

A burst of energy came at them.

All three sisters ducked.

More blasts of light shot towards them.

Nyx narrowed her eyes at the treeline. "Looks like dragons aren't the only thing that came through."

"We have a Dragon Guard running around." Niamh

threw one of her knives. The blade whizzed through the air and embedded in the man's throat. Blood gurgled from his mouth.

More blasts of light came at them. Another guard lay just beyond the trees.

Niamh palmed another knife, then yelped when a blast hit her arm.

The red dragon's amber eyes opened, and it blew a plume of fire at the guard. The man screamed as the blast blew his body apart.

"We should go." Nyx grabbed her sisters' arms.

Niamh yanked her arm away and hit the dragon's snout when it drew closer. "Back off, beast. Come near us and I will take you down."

"Niamh, you don't hit dragons," Nyx hissed. "Are you trying to get us all killed?" She didn't know if her magic would be much defence against dragon fire and didn't want to find out.

"Agreed. Dragons are noble creatures and take offence to —" Novia said.

To Nyx's amazement, the dragon bowed its head to Niamh.

Niamh frowned. "What's it doing?"

"It's showing a sign of respect." Nyx furrowed her brow.

"The creature's spirit doesn't feel broken." Novia patted its head. "Poor thing, I dread to think what kind of abuse it's gone through at the hands of the Dragon Guard. Maybe we should help the dragons. Find somewhere safe for them. It would be better than forcing them back through the shield."

Niamh rolled her eyes. "Sister, we have enough problems to deal with without taking care of a bunch of fire breathers."

"But we could use them, they would come in handy," Novia insisted. "We'd have more dragons to fight with and more protection against the Archdruid and the Dragon Guard."

Nyx reached out to Darius with her mind and felt... Nothing.

Druid?

No answer came.

Darius?

Panic washed over her. "I can't sense Darius. Something is wrong." She unfurled her wings and took off, hovering above them. "Look around to see if you can find him. If there are more guards, try to contain them. We might be able to make use of them later."

"Contain them?" Niamh scoffed. "Are you mad? What good will a Dragon Guard do us? We can't use them as leverage. The Archdruid would sooner kill them than let us use them for negotiations."

"Just do it." Nyx rose higher and scanned the ground around them.

Nothing.

"Hey, we can't fly," Niamh called out to her.

The red dragon crouched in front of them. *Fly.*

Niamh, the dragon wants you to climb on, Nyx said.

Why? Niamh took a step back, as if afraid.

I don't know. I think he likes you, but doesn't communicate very well. Climb on.

I'm not sensing a threat from him. Novia sounded excited. *Let's go.*

Niamh hesitated. *Me? Fly? I'm not Nyx. I prefer my feet on the ground.*

It likes you. Come on. Novia gave her a shove towards the dragon.

I thought you were supposed to be the docile one in this sisterhood,

61

Niamh grumbled.

I'd love to have a dragon choose me. Embrace it.

Her sisters clambered onto the dragon. The red beast rose and hovered near Nyx.

"This is incredible." Novia grinned.

"This is terrifying!" Niamh screeched and clutched the dragon's neck tighter. "I want to get down. Gods, why did I let you talk me into this?"

We can cover more ground from the air. Just give the dragon commands with your mind, Nyx told them.

I can't communicate with it. That's not how my power works, Niamh protested.

You can learn to. Nyx flew off and glided over the abandoned buildings. Below, she spotted another dragon. The black beast glanced up at her and sent out a plume of fire.

She raised her hand and deflected it. Wonderful. As if they didn't have enough to deal with already.

First the Archdruid, escaped prisoners, now rogue dragons. But the question was, where was Darius, and why couldn't she sense him anymore?

"Nyx!" someone called out to her.

She narrowed her eyes and spotted Ranelle and Lucien just outside the shield.

Good gods, how had they ended up here?

Go, keep looking around for Darius and roundup any Dragon Guards, she told her sisters.

Nyx swooped down. The dragon advanced towards her.

"Stop that!" Light pulsed from her hand exploded in front of the dragon. The beast whimpered and backed away.

Nyx glanced at her hand. Why had she done that? She rarely lost control of her powers now.

"Thank the gods we found you." Ranelle pressed herself

against the shield. "Hurry, let us through. There are guards everywhere."

"Why are you both here?" She furrowed her brow. "What happened? How did you get here?"

"The Archdruid sent the Dragon Guard to arrest us," Lucien replied. "I sensed them coming and fled to get Ranelle. It's not safe for us either. We flew here with Darius."

She raised Ambrose's staff again, but the shield still refused to open. "I can't let you through. Hurry, you two need to get out of here and find somewhere safe to hide."

"Why would the Dragon Guard want us? I don't understand." Ranelle shook her head.

"Because you're Darius' friends. The Archdruid will use anyone he can against us." Nyx ran a hand through her hair. "Darius came through the shield, but I can't sense him. I'm afraid something has happened to him."

"Why won't the shield open?" Lucien pressed his hands against it.

Nyx shook her head. "I don't know. Please, I will try and come and get you as soon as I figure out a way to open the shield again."

"Maybe Darius didn't come through either. We will search for him out here as well. Let's hope that shield stays up," Ranelle remarked.

She took a deep breath and nodded. Now all she could do was hope.

CHAPTER 9

"I don't like this." Niamh winced at every movement of the dragon's body. "Why does this thing choose me? You're the one that communes with animals."

She couldn't understand why the dragon would choose her for anything. She wasn't much of an animal lover. Most animals usually feared her. Perhaps she shouldn't have hit it and should have listened to her sisters. The creature needed to learn some respect. If it dared harm one of her sisters, she would make it sorry.

The forest stretched out below them in a blanket of green and brown. Further up, shimmered the churning waters of the river. Waves crashed and pounded against the embankment.

"You should be happy. Having a dragon choose you is rare and an incredible thing." Novia grinned as she gripped Niamh's waist. "Be honoured by that. I would love to have a dragon of my own."

"I'm not looking for a pet. You can have this one if you want him. Not sure I like the idea of having a bunch of dragons around." She had been uncomfortable enough around Darius' dragon. "Besides, I thought you already had your own dragon?" Novia had told them about the dragon she'd seen in the temple, but Niamh wondered if she'd imagined it since the elusive dragon hadn't appeared since.

"I think you have a connection with each other. I can

sense it. How else could you hear him? He wants you to be his rider."

"What kind of connection?" Niamh frowned. "I'm not Nyx. I don't have some odd druid magic in me. And I don't go around chatting with animals all the time. We have more important things to worry about."

"We are half druid. It makes sense we might have similar abilities."

"I'm a mind whisperer, not a druid." Niamh didn't want to think of herself as a druid. Their father was a killer — little more than a mindless slave. At least there had been a reason for the people she'd killed.

They flew further away from the towering buildings that stood close to the palace. Trees spread out in a dense green and gold blanket.

"How or why would I have a connection to this?" Niamh motioned to the dragon. *Is Nyx's connection to her druid affecting us?*

We are bonded. Another voice rang through her mind.

She narrowed her eyes and leaned forward to stare into the dragon's glowing amber eyes. *I'm having a private conversation with my sister. Stay out of my head.*

"Bonded how?" Novia asked out loud.

I am her animas. I have been with her since birth.

"My what?" Niamh asked. "You haven't been with me since birth. I've never met you."

You don't remember me.

She snorted. *I don't remember anything before the age of ten. Why is that?*

We were separated after the city fell.

"This is incredible. The two of you must have been connected to each other for years. I wish I could find my dragon again." Novia sighed.

"None of this makes sense." She shook her head. "Why

would we have some kind of animal attached to us? It's ridiculous. Stop letting your dream of having a dragon cloud your judgement."

Novia needed to get over all of this nonsense. How could she have some kind of spirit animal? And if she did, wouldn't she remember it? Or at least feel some kind of connection to it?

She didn't know what to feel towards the creature. Other than terrified. She would never envy Nyx's ability to fly again. Flying was too petrifying. Any moment they could fall out of the sky and fall to their deaths.

"We lost a lot when we were children. Maybe he's something else you lost. Think about it, we were the queen's daughters. It's not impossible to think we might have had these creatures to befriend and protect us."

Niamh scoffed. "Keep on dreaming, sister. Even if they are connected to us, it doesn't mean we're going to keep them."

"We can't turn them away. He's a part of you, and you will need to take care of each other."

Niamh laughed. How had she ended up with a dragon as some kind of pet?

"I think the lack of air up here has addled your brain."

Novia snorted. "My mind is clear. Do you have a name, dragon?"

The guards called me Dragon Six.

Niamh, you should give him a new name. Something meaningful. Something to make him yours.

No. If you love him so much, you take care of him. I don't have the time or energy for such responsibility. She turned away from her sister. "We need to focus on finding the druid. Six, fly lower."

Novia thumped her shoulder. *Six? Aren't you going to give him a better name?*

This isn't my dragon and we have work to do. If you want to make friends, go ahead. She had heard enough nonsense. Niamh swung her leg over this side of the moving dragon and jumped.

Novia cried out an alarm, "Niamh!"

She ignored her and raised her arms to control her fall. She couldn't fly, but she could levitate. Tree branches thwacked against her as she fell. Raising her arms further, she swerved around them. Spotting the vacant branch, she landed with a thud.

A red mass swooped down and landed on the branch above.

Niamh groaned. *Quiet, I sense something.* She held out her hand. She didn't have the patience to deal with Six. Why the dragon thought he had a bond with her, she couldn't fathom. Having a dragon around would only lead to more problems.

Novia jumped down and landed beside her. *Sense what?*

Listen with your mind.

I don't hear anything.

She repressed a sigh. *Concentrate.*

Novia flinched. *You don't like me, do you?*

Quiet. Niamh gave her a shove. *Look.* Below them, something stalked through the shadows.

What is that? Novia leaned forward.

Niamh gave her a hard look. What would it take to get her to shut up?

A shadow moved through the trees. Swift and silent. She narrowed her eyes, and the forest came into clear view. Something remained cloaked. Whatever it was set her senses on edge.

Dragon, why don't you jump down and see what that is down there? The beast might as well be good for something. It would be better if she and Novia didn't get hurt.

Six swooped down, a blur of muscle and glowing red scales, and someone cried out an alarm.

Niamh leapt and landed on a lower branch.

"Get this thing off me!"

Six pinned down a dark-haired woman with pointed ears. Most of her body was covered by the massive dragon.

Niamh guessed she must be some sort of fae, judging by her ears. Her senses didn't tell her anything else about the woman.

Novia came over and gasped. "Six, get away from her. She is an Ilari."

Six screamed as the woman wrapped her hands around his neck. Smoke billowed around the dragon and his screams grew louder. Niamh winced as his pain tore through her mind.

The screams grew louder as memory dragged her in. She clutched a red dragon to her chest as the walls around them trembled.

She stomped forward; hand outstretched as the memory faded. "Six, come to me."

Light flared around the dragon as he shifted into a smaller form. So small he wrapped himself around Niamh and almost knocked her over.

I don't want to go to sleep again. Don't leave me. Six clung to her tighter.

Niamh wrapped an arm around the dragon. *It's alright, you won't be taken from me again.* The dragon relaxed against her and curled itself around her neck, growling at the woman who'd attacked him. "A death fae?" She had heard of such creatures that came from outside the lower realm, but had never encountered one.

Ilari were rare and kept to themselves. Other magickind despised them because a mere touch from them could cause death. Legend also said they could bring the dead

68

back to life; she never knew if that was true or not.

"Why are *you* attacking me?" the woman demanded. "I haven't done anything." She scrambled up. She wore a short top that covered her chest but left her arms and midriff bare. Along with a short skirt with sandals. Luminescent silver tattoos covered almost every part of her skin. "Who are you?"

"We are —" Novia began.

"No one. Why are you skulking around in the shadows?" Niamh stepped between her sister and the Ilari. *Don't tell her anything about who we are. We can't trust her.*

If we're stuck here, shouldn't we try to get to know the people? Novia arched a brow.

No. Not when they're death fae. We can't trust anyone.

"I was minding my own business." The woman crossed her arms. "You two don't look like Outsiders."

"Who or what are Outsiders?" Novia furrowed her brow.

Niamh scanned the Ilari with her senses to get a read on her. Was the Ilari immune to her powers and if so, how?

The woman's eyes flashed. "You're using magic on me." She took a step forward.

Six growled and shot a column of fire at the Ilari. The woman yelped and ducked for cover. She glowered at them. "Who are you people? Dragons don't live inside the shield. You come from the outside world, don't you?"

"Who we are isn't your business." Niamh glared back at the woman. "Stay away from us. If you don't, it'll be the last thing you'll ever do." *Let's go.* She motioned for Novia to follow.

Six jumped off her shoulder, unperturbed by what the death fae had done to him. Light flashed around him again as he shifted back into his enormous form.

They scrambled back onto the dragon and flew off.

"I think I remembered something when the Ilari used her magic on Six." She patted the dragon. "He was mine. I saw a glimpse of us together. But I don't know what it means or where we were. Six, do you remember what happened to us when we were children? Did we die?"

I don't remember what happened after the city fell. I woke up outside the shield and couldn't remember much of anything.

"See, I was right. You are connected to each other. But we shouldn't make an Ilari our enemy," Novia remarked. "We need allies if we're going to be stuck in."

"We're not allying ourselves with her. How did you know what she was?"

"Because I met a lot of different magic kind on Glenfel. Guess I'm not as naïve as you thought."

She winced. "I never said you were, but you need to be careful."

"There's nothing wrong with being polite to people. Politeness works better than being rude. Even on the toughest prisoners." Novia gripped her waist tighter as Six glided over the expanse of forest. "Do you think she was one of the queen's prisoners?"

Niamh shrugged. "I guess, but who are the Outsiders she mentioned?" She scanned the forest with her senses. Minds buzzed around her. She sensed Nyx not too far away. *Six, can you sense my other sister?*

Yes.

Good, head for her.

Six banked sharply to the left.

See, he's not so bad, is he? Novia nudged her.

Niamh sighed. "I guess not. I couldn't read the Ilari."

"Neither could I. She must be immune to our powers."

"I don't like people who are immune. That makes them unpredictable."

"Not everyone can be read. It's better to get to know

people than to learn everything about them through magic."

Six swooped lower until Nyx came into view.

"Any sign of Darius?" Niamh slid off the dragon and walked over to her other sister.

Nyx shook her head. "No, I don't understand. Why can't I sense him anymore? We're connected."

"Maybe something happened to him. Perhaps he is unconscious."

"Niamh." Novia shot her a glare.

"What?" She'd only stated a possibility.

Nyx winced. "I'd know if he were unconscious. I would sense it. He's just gone."

"I doubt a fall would kill him. We'll find him, but we need to be on our guard. We already found a death fae and there's another group called the Outsiders who live somewhere nearby. This place won't be as safe as we thought."

CHAPTER 10

Novia breathed in the scents of the forest. Pinecones, fresh grass. She didn't get much of that on Glenfel since it was only a small island. "Andre, are you there? If you are, please come out." Her heart pounded as she stepped inside.

The high arched stone walls loomed over her. Wet and decaying leaves covered the dirty flagstone floor and ancient vines covered the bare grey stone walls. Not much remained of the temple aside from a circular altar that stood in the centre of the room. Half melted candles sat there from where the queen had last performed a ritual. Novia shuddered at the memory.

She wanted to run as far away from this place as possible, but she thought Andre might have come back here. She still had no idea why he disappeared after he'd taken her back to the palace.

"You don't need to be afraid. I won't hurt you. Neither will my sisters."

She froze as a howling sound echoed through the empty temple.

Conjuring up a large orb of light, she took a deep breath. *I can do this. I'm not going to let bad memories stop me again.* Casting her senses out, she scanned the temple with her mind.

Nothing came to her.

Andre had to be somewhere. Maybe with his help, she

could cover more ground in the search for Darius. The other dragons followed her commands, but she didn't have the same connection to them as she did with Andre.

"Have you found anything?"

Novia jumped as Nyx, riding Ember, flew over.

She blew out a breath. "Must you startle me?" She scowled.

"Don't look at me like that. Niamh scowls enough for two people. What are you doing? We already searched here."

"I know. I am…looking for Andre. I thought he'd come back here."

"The dragon? Are you sure it wasn't just an escaped prisoner?"

Novia's scowl deepened. "You and Niamh have dragons."

"And I'm not saying you don't have one. Just Six and Ember didn't run away. Plus, there's so many strange creatures in this city." Nyx climbed off her dragon. *Ember, can you find Andre?*

He's afraid, Ember replied.

"What?" Novia was relieved Nyx allowed her the listen in through her mind.

The guards tortured Five and Six the most. Five is weak. Six was strong and stubborn, like Niamh.

Novia crossed her arms. "Andre isn't weak. And don't call him Five anymore. What those guards did to all of you was barbaric."

"Let's keep looking. I'm sure Andre will come back to you soon."

Novia backed away from the temple and shivered. "Can we destroy this place?"

Nyx's eyes widened. "Why?"

"Because everything about it reminds me of her." She

shuddered even thinking of the queen. "Besides, it's a ruin. We should get rid of it and make way for something new." Light flared between her fingers and she hurtled against the wall. The light exploded against the stone, sending bits of rock flying.

A shadow flew over them as Niamh and Six swooped down. "We have a problem."

Novia sighed. "Another one?"

What had gone wrong now? Another dragon? More guards or former prisoners roaming around?

"Some of the grass near the shield is scorched. The shield is weakening. We need to do something to get the Dragon Guard to back off."

Nyx shook her head. "We can't go back through the shield. If we could, maybe I could sense my druid. I hope Ranelle and Lucien are safe, too."

"Maybe the three of us could get through. Novia, have you found your dragon yet?" Niamh turned to her.

She shook her head. "Not yet. He's hiding from me. Maybe Six and Ember can —"

"Baron," Niamh corrected.

"Excuse me?"

"His name is Baron. You said I should give him a new name, so I have. Named him after a man who once helped me."

"Right. *Baron* and Ember could join their powers with ours."

"Call him with your mind," Nyx suggested. "Reassure him."

Andre, come here. Please. I just want to know you're safe.

Something whimpered, and a grey-skinned dragon stalked out of the shadows of the temple.

Baron and Ember rushed over to him and rubbed their heads against him.

74

"You're here." Novia ran over and wrapped her arms around him. "Why did you run away from me?"

Weak. Not enough strength. Andre rested his head against her.

The guards didn't let us feed, Ember said. *We need energy from the earth. They put runes on us and forced us to stay in this form. But they are fading. The runes have to be renewed every few days.*

We need a line of energy, Baron said. *Druids and Fae can draw energy from Erthea.*

"Energy? How?" Niamh frowned.

"He means lines of energy that run through the earth. Maybe I can draw one out." Nyx raised her hand, but nothing happened.

"How does it work?" Niamh took hold of Nyx and Novia's hands.

"Darius usually reaches for energy and compels it to open. That's what I'm doing." Nyx blew out a breath.

The sisters cast their senses out, reaching out into the earth. Her senses became stronger and more heightened when she joined powers with them. Like they were one. In some ways, they were. Three parts of a whole. The part she'd lost eight years ago.

A glowing line of white energy appeared.

"Pretty," Novia breathed.

"Won't they need more than a trickle of energy?" Niamh asked.

Rise higher, Novia thought. *We need to call forth more energy.* She and Niamh raised their free hands. Light exploded as energy rippled through the vein of energy.

All three dragons jumped about as if splashing in water. The sisters laughed as light washed over them.

Novia wrapped an arm around her dragon. "See, I told you they were ours."

"But why don't we remember them?" Niamh jumped

when Baron bumped into her and wrapped his body around hers.

"Probably because someone erased all our memories. Someone powerful. Why else would we have been split up?" Nyx asked.

Each dragon shifted into different animals.

We can shift! Ember, now in the form of a large black wolf, licked Nyx's face, and almost knocked her over. *I haven't shifted in a century.*

Andre shifted into a grey cat with long fur and Baron into a large falcon, spreading his wings and landing on Niamh's shoulder.

"Maybe we can use them to track Darius." Nyx took hold of their hands again. The vibrations around them became stronger.

The buzz of minds from the Outsides grew louder. But no sign of Darius.

"Maybe he didn't make it through the shield." Novia squeezed her hand. "You can't be sure if he did or not."

"I have no way of knowing unless we can get back through the shield." Nyx's shoulders slumped. "There must be a way to get through again. Ambrose used to come and go from the city all the time. He would know how to get through."

"I doubt he'll be coming back." Novia scowled.

Novia couldn't say she had much love for their father, either. He had been the one who had taken her from Glenfel and handed her over to the queen. What he had done was unforgivable.

"If our dragons — animals — are spirits, why can't they go through the shield?" Niamh motioned off into the distance. "Spirits can go anywhere, can't they?"

Novia shook her head. "They can't enter Glenfel or leave the island. The Archdruid created wards and spells to keep them out and if anyone died on the island, they would be stuck there."

"One of them could look for Darius and check to see how things are going back in Alaris. Ranelle and Lucien are still there," Nyx said. "The Archdruid might use them against us."

I'll go. Ember shifted into a small dragon, barely the size of a hunting dog. *I can get through.*

"But what if you get captured again?" Novia frowned. "The Dragon Guard could take you, then learn there is a way through."

"Maybe these will help." Nyx traced several glowing runes around Ember's neck. "I think these are protection."

"You think? How do you know what they are?" Niamh scoffed.

"I don't know. They just come to me sometimes. Go, Ember. Be careful."

I will. The dragon roared, then took to the air. Light flashed as Ember slammed against the shield.

Novia winced as pain reverberated through her head. She guessed her sisters and their animals were connected.

"You need to be incorporeal," Nyx told her dragon. "Become energy."

I haven't turned into energy in many years. Ember shook his head at her.

Draw energy from us if you have to.

Light flared around the dragon as he transformed into glowing orbs of light that passed through the shield.

All three sisters come to the ground with Baron and Andre.

That had taken a lot more energy than Novia had expected.

Novia ground when she opened her eyes.

She blinked and fed her sisters and their dragons

slumped beside them.

"Nyx? Niamh?" She shook them.

Arrows whizz towards them as someone fired from the trees.

Novia screamed as she blurred out of the way. She stumbled and hit the ground. Fatigue weighed on her like a heavy blanket.

Andre leapt into the air and knocked someone to the ground.

Someone cried out an alarm. A male elf. His long blonde hair fell past his shoulders, pointed ears stuck out, and his green eyes narrowed on them.

"Why are you shooting at us?" Novia glanced over at her still-unconscious sisters.

"Because you're trespassing on our territory." The elf shoved Andre away from him. "Strangers aren't welcome here. Get out or we'll kill you all."

CHAPTER 11

Nyx couldn't sleep that night. The room she'd picked had a large fourposter bed. Blue linens come with the bed and the walls were blue with silver filigree leaves around them. She hated not waking up next to Darius. The bed felt empty without him. Maybe she'd grown a little too used to his presence.

Too bad Ember wasn't here to keep her company. Her sisters had their own chambers down the hall.

Damn it, druid, where are you? Why can't I feel you anymore? She pushed her long hair off her face. Worse still, she didn't even have anything of his to help find him with. Or to use in summoning spells. Aside from Sirin. But using spells with her hadn't helped, either.

Nyx scrambled out of bed. Someone whispered at the edge of her mind, but it sounded too faint for her to make out the voice or the words.

Now what?

Druid?

No reply came.

Maybe not Darius. There were too many strange things in the old city to be sure. She headed out of the chamber to where crystal torches lit the hall in a faint green ethereal glow. Shadows danced along the wall and she shivered.

It was doubtful this place would ever feel like home.

She went back to her chamber and grabbed some slippers she had found earlier and put them on before heading out again.

Novia's door stood wide open.

"Nov?" Odd, Novia always insisted on keeping her door locked at night. Nyx knew she did it to try and feel safe.

The chamber beyond lay empty. The four-poster bed had its linens upturned and half hanging off. Clothes and other items lay strewn across the flagstone floor. That was unlike Novia, who always insisted on keeping everything in order.

"Andre, are you here?" Her eyes took a moment to adjust to the darkness.

Andre, in his small dragon form, huddled in the corner.

"Where's Novia?" She opened the door to the latrine but found no one there either.

The dragon didn't respond. Nyx knelt in front of him. "Andre, you're safe here." She scanned the palace for her sister but didn't find her. Curse it. Her powers were still weak from sending Ember through the shield.

She sent out waves of reassurance to Andre and prayed he would calm down enough to talk to her.

The dragon huffed and whined. *She's here. She never left…*

"Good. Where is she?" Nyx furrowed her brow. "Why can't I sense her?" She placed her hand on his head. Her eyes snapped shut.

Lyra stood outside the temple's ground. "Look at me! I'm stuck in this body! Everything I've worked for is ruined." No, not Lyra. The queen…

"This isn't my fault, Evony. I had to do something," Ambrose snapped.

"Do you hate me so much you had the Archdruid murderer our children?" she snarled.

Ambrose looked away, and his jaw tightened. "We need to bury the girls. Then —"

"You bury them. You're the one who killed them." Evony glanced back at the fallen bodies of Nyx and her sisters. Three small dragons lay curled around them, covered in blood.

Evony raised her hand and blasted all three dragons away. "You were supposed to protect my children," she growled at them. "Worthless beasts." A ball of light formed between her fingers.

"Don't you think there's been enough bloodshed?"

She winced as the memory faded and Andre's fear washed over her like icy water. "You didn't mean Novia, did you? Oh, gods." Light shimmered around her, then faded. "Curse my stupid weak powers."

Niamh, wake up!

Her sister didn't reply. Nyx knew she didn't have time to go and wake her. She had to get to Novia.

She ran down the hall. "Keeper, are you there?"

The keeper flashed into existence. "Yes?"

"Can you transport me outside?"

"I cannot. Only inside the palace walls. The palace's wards are draining all the energy in the palace."

Wonderful, something else she had to worry about. It would have to wait.

When she reached the end of the hall, she stared out of the high arched window that looked over the outer courtyard. Below, Novia stood next to the well where the queen lay trapped.

Oh, holy spirits, was Novia going to let her out?

"Novia, stop!" She pounded against the glass and pressed her face against the window.

Novia didn't acknowledge her and kept throwing things at the barrier that stood over the well.

Curse it. If Novia broke the queen out, their lives would be over.

Running down they would take too long.

She raised her hand and a few sparks of energy rippled against the window. That would do no good. A blade formed from the bracelet Darius had given her. It slammed against the glass but didn't crack it.

This is going to hurt. Nyx hoped this would work, but it would do some serious damage. She pulled her wings back and ran at the window.

Glass shattered as she threw herself against it. Wind rushed past her as she fell in a shower of glass. Screaming, she unfurled her wings, flapping hard to gain some momentum.

She hit the ground hard. Air rushed from her lungs. Cuts covered her arms, hands and legs and face.

"Novia, stop this!" Nyx ignored her bleeding cuts as she grabbed her sister's arm. "What are doing? You can't let her out."

"But I must obey my mistress."

Oh no. How could the queen have got into Novia's mind?

"You have to stop. You know you can't release her. Have you forgotten what she did to you?" Nyx knew Novia must be under the queen's control. Novia didn't want to let the queen out.

Laughter echoed from inside the well. "At least she has the good sense to help me," the queen snarled.

"Only because you're forcing her to."

"One of you will let me out. I'm not spending another minute in this cesspit." The queen hurled an energy ball at the barrier.

"I must help my mistress." Novia turned away from her.

What would it take to get her sister to snap out of this?

Gripping Novia's wrist, she released her power. Energy pulse through her but didn't reverberate through the air like it usually did.

More laughter.

"You're not strong enough to break my hold on her."

"Oh, do shut up," Niamh snapped as she landed beside Nyx and stared at Novia. "Please tell me she's not under the witch's control."

"I must help my mistress," Novia repeated.

Niamh groaned. "What do we do?"

"My powers are too weak to work on her," Nyx whispered. "Hit her. Knock her out."

Niamh's eyes went wide. "But —"

"Do it. I can't." She held up her hands.

"Sis, I am truly sorry about this." Novia threw back her arm, hitting Novia to the ground.

Nyx flinched. "I didn't mean that hard. I hope you didn't break anything."

"Now, what do we do with her?"

"No!" the queen screamed. "You —"

"Ignore her." Nyx stepped towards the well.

"Don't go near that. Dripping with blood, you might set her free given how strong blood magic can be." Niamh put out her arm to stop her. "I'll check." She knelt by the barrier. "It looks intact. The druid would know if —"

Nyx ripped off a piece of her nightgown to bandage her hand and wrapped the fabric around it. "It will hold. We need to get Novia somewhere secure."

"I'm not sure I can carry her by myself." Niamh whistled and Baron flew down. "Baron, carry Novia." She turned to Nyx. "Why did you jump out the window?"

"Had to. My powers are weak."

Niamh scowled. "Mine, too. I hope Ember got through. Come on, we need to get her locked up and your cuts need tending to. Where shall we put her?"

"You want to lock her up?" Nyx gasped.

"It's the only way to keep her safe. Unless you have a better idea?"

She shook her head. "I don't. Guess we'll have to keep her locked up until we can figure out how to release her."

"Should we try the dungeon?"

"Let's lock her in her chamber for now."

"Bad idea. She could easily get out again."

Nyx swayed on her feet. "Fine, let's sleep next to her and lock ourselves in."

Niamh helped her up to their old bedchamber that had once been the nursery.

"Why are we in here?" Nyx frowned. "We could have just used Novia's chamber."

"Because it's bigger, and the door has proper wards on it." Niamh heaved Novia onto the first bed, chained a shackle to Novia's wrist, and attached it to the bedpost.

"I'm afraid to ask where you got that from."

"I carry it everywhere. The first rule in the Order of Blood is to be prepared for anything." Niamh rummaged through her pack.

"Is Novia alright?"

"She's fine. Aside from a sore nose and the bad head she'll have in the morning. I know how to hit people without breaking things." Niamh pulled out two jars. "Have you got any glass stuck in your cuts?" Nyx shrugged. "Next time you jump through a window, use your nightdress to shield yourself." Niamh raised her hand. "*Brinshee.*"

She cried out as shards of glass flew onto the floor. "Ow. How did you do that?"

"Elvish magic. I learnt about healing in the Order." Niamh rubbed a salve over the cuts and bandage the worst of them.

"Thanks." Nyx rubbed her wrists. "Now we need to —"

"Sleep. You're exhausted. We all are. We'll deal with little sister in the morning."

"But —"

"No buts. We'll be useless if we're too tired to fight. Baron and Andre are here. They'll alert us if they hear anything."

Nyx shook her head. "I can't sleep. Because…"

"Because your druid isn't here?" Niamh asked.

She nodded. "That and because I'm afraid I'll have more nightmares of being buried. Or worse. What if the queen tries to control me?"

"The queen isn't touching us. She'll have to go through me first. Tomorrow, we'll work on dealing with her." Niamh climbed on the bed beside her and Novia then slipped her arms around them both. "I'm not losing either of you."

Nyx buried her face against her sister's shoulder. "I'm glad you're here."

"We're sisters and nothing — especially not our mother — is going to come between us." Niamh sniffed. "I know I seem tough, but I get scared too. I don't want to lose either of you."

Nyx put her arms around her. "You won't."

CHAPTER 12

Bright white light dragged Darius through the shield. Then he found himself falling. His magic failed him and no one answered his call for help. Icy water enveloped Darius, and darkness threatened to drag him under.

He fought to stay conscious and struggled to swim to the surface. He reached for magic to draw air, but the more he called for it, the further it receded. Why wouldn't his power come to him?

Darius kicked his legs, but he couldn't get any closer to the surface. The current pounded against him, forcing him backwards. He raised his hand to call the elements to him. To control water and summon a bubble of air. The cuff his father had put on him flashed with light. Bit by bit, his power drained away from him. Holy spirits, his father had rendered him powerless. The more magic he used, the more he'd lose.

He tugged against the cuff. *Nyx?* He reached out to her with his mind. Talking in thought required less power, and he needed her help. Darius fought harder as he swam against the current. *Nyx, can you hear me?*

She didn't reply and he couldn't feel her presence either. *Sirin?* Maybe he could summon his dragon instead. If someone heard him, he'd have help.

No answer came.

Something swam towards him. He couldn't make out much in the murkiness of the river. Other than the glow of eyes and shimmer of a long tail.

Oh no. Why did there have to be a creature here? He had to be in the old city now. There shouldn't be any magickind here.

Something grabbed hold of his ankles and yanked him downwards. Holy spirits, he had to get to the surface. His lungs burned for air. Darius called up more magic and yet again it leaked away. His sword and other weapons had been taken when he was dragged to the palace. So he had nothing to fight with.

He tugged at the cuff, but it wouldn't budge. *Nyx, please hear me. Sirin?* He thought about calling Ranelle or Lucien, but he couldn't be sure if they had got through the shield.

Still nothing. He wasn't going to die here. Using his free leg, he kicked against whatever held him. Finally, it released its grip. Darius kicked harder, and the surface drew nearer. Something caught hold of his ankles and pulled him down. Blackness enveloped his vision and finally dragged him under.

He woke up to the faint sound of singing and the murmur of voices. Light shimmered around the dimly lit space. He lay against something hard.

"Good, you're awake." A young woman swam around him. Her silvery hair flowed around her pale face. Her chest was bare except for a metal breastplate that covered her breasts and circled around her ribs. Her skin shimmered like moonlight. A long blue tail floated behind her.

Darius blinked a few times; sure he was dreaming. Not a woman, a mermaid. How could she be here? Merfolk never came this far inland, and they lived in the sea, not in a river.

"Where — where am I?" His voice came out raspy, but he could still speak and breathe. A bubble of air shimmered around his head.

"I thought you drowned. Most land walkers do. It's so annoying." She rolled her eyes. "So I conjured a bubble. I figured you'd need it."

Darius gasped for more air. His hands and feet were bound with reeds. The water kept him upright. "Why am I bound? Who are you?" he demanded. "Since when do mermaids live in a river?"

"I'm Azura. I don't have much choice about living here. If I hadn't grabbed you, you'd be dead by now."

"Why am I bound?"

"Because I'm trying to decide whether to trade you to the Outsiders or not." She touched his cheek. "You are handsome. Maybe I should keep you around for my amusement."

He drew away from her touch. "I already have a lifemate and she'll be looking for me. So I suggest you let me get to the surface." He tugged at the reeds, but they wouldn't break. "Who are the Outsiders?"

She laughed, then her mouth fell open. "You don't know?"

"No, I'm not from round here."

"How can you not be? The river curves all the way around and everywhere is blocked by the wall of light. Or did the queen drag you in here as a prisoner? Where do you come from?"

"That's not important. I need to go. My lifemate and my friends need me. They're in trouble."

"How did you get here, then?"

"That's… Not important. Now let me go!" He never called Nyx his lifemate before. The idea didn't sound so bad. She meant everything to him. One way or another, he had to get back to her.

Were Ranelle and Lucien safe? Had they got through the shield? Had the shield faltered? So many questions raced through his mind.

"No, not until you tell me where you come from. I never get to travel through the shield very often — not unless the queen allows it."

Darius sighed. "There's not much to tell. What do you mean, the queen allows you?"

"Everyone trapped in the city is a prisoner of the queen. How can you not know about her?" Azura's eyes widened.

"How many people were trapped here?"

She shrugged. "A couple of hundred, perhaps. Most of them don't like me or my crew."

Darius furrowed his brow. "How long have you been trapped here? A hundred years or less?"

Azura laughed. "A hundred years? I'm not *that* old. I don't know how long I've been here. The queen took me prisoner when I was around twelve years old. I've lived here and on land within the boundary of the city since then. I can't go beyond the river because the glowing wall stopped me." She scowled. "I only get to see the outside world when the queen allows me through the shield."

His mind raced. How could he convince her to let him go? They were too deep for him to swim. He couldn't swim whilst bound, nor did he have magic to aid him.

"What were those loud noises and bright flashes I saw in the sky?" Azura persisted. "Tell me. Was someone trying to get through the shield?"

Coldness seeped through his skin. His shirt was long gone, along with his boots. His trousers provided little warmth. "My body is losing heat. I'll die unless you take me to the surface."

"You haven't told me anything." Her eyes flashed. "Can you open the shield? Tell me!"

Unconsciousness threatened to drag him under again.

"I could if you let me get on dry land and get warm."

"If I take you to land, you will use magic against me." She swam around him. "What are those strange marks on your skin? They look like runes, but I don't recognise them."

"They are symbols of…" He fought to keep his eyes open.

"Of what?" She slapped his face. "You can't be falling asleep again already."

The force did little good to keep him alert. Azura grumbled and slapped him harder. The water around him grew warmer.

"See this cuff on my wrist? If you take it off, I'll tell you whatever you want to know."

"Really?" She brightened.

"Yes. Just keep me warm. So I can stay conscious." The water around him grew warmer.

She swam close and yanked at the cuff on his wrist. If you could get her to put it on, maybe he could use it to drain her power. His magic would be weak, but he should have enough to get to the surface. She pulled harder. "Why when it comes off?" Azura scowled. "Are you trying to trick me, land walker?"

"I'm a druid. Damn it, it should come off."

"A druid? Do you know Taliesin?"

"Taliesin?" Darius furrowed his brow. The name sounded familiar, but he couldn't place it.

Where did he know that name from? He knew he had heard it somewhere before. Perhaps his father had mentioned it.

"He's my friend. I don't get to spend as much time with him now. He's too busy helping the Outsiders."

"Who are the Outsiders?"

"People who live in the forest. They come to fish in the river. I trade with them sometimes. Most of them are wary of me and my crew."

Darius wondered who the crew that she kept mentioning was. were they nearby? What would they do with him?

He took a deep breath to try and keep himself awake. "But who are they? How long have they been here?"

She shrugged. "How should I know? They have been here as long as I can remember."

"Can we go to see Taliesin? I'd like to meet him." Maybe talking to another druid would be helpful. If he could keep his true identity a secret, Taliesin might be able to convince Azura to let him go.

"He doesn't come to visit often."

"Can you call him in thought?"

She shook her head. "He can't communicate in thought."

He suppressed a groan. "At least get this cuff off me."

"Why? What does it do?"

"I — I promised it to you, didn't I? There must be a way to get it off."

Azura pulled at it again. Then she swam away and rummaged through a pile of discarded items. Something silver flashed as she pulled out a sword. "Pretty, isn't it? I took it from one of the Outsiders."

"How will that help? It can't cut through metal."

"No, but it will take your hand off." Azura raised her blade.

"No, don't do that!"

"Why not? How can I get it off? You don't need to worry about losing it. I'm sure you can use magic to stick it back on."

"My hands are bound. You can't cut it off."

She furrowed her brow. "Fine." She cut through the reeds around his arms.

Darius flexed his wrists and tugged at the cuff. "Maybe you should cut my hand off, but I'll need you to bind the wound after."

He could preserve his hand and reattach it once he had his magic back.

"Are you sure?" Her brow furrowed.

"It might be the only way to get it off. But take me to the surface to do it. I'll show you how to call Taliesin in thought."

"Why can't you do that here? And I told you, Taliesin can't be contacted in thought."

"Because it needs to be done on the surface. And all druids are taught to communicate in thought."

"Fine." She grabbed hold of him. "Let's go. My crew will know what to do with you." Azura grabbed him and dragged him out of the wreck.

"Where are we going?" Darius struggled as she raised her hands and reeds bound themselves around his wrists. He couldn't believe she had bound him again. He didn't have the strength to swim or fight against her.

"To see my crew."

The current churned against them, silt and other debris hitting him, along with the churning tide. Azura cursed a few times as she dragged him along. Something like covered above the surface. It took a few moments for him to realise it was a ship. The vessel appeared smaller than most of the ships that came in and out of Andovia. Why was it here?

Then he remembered Azura had said she could only leave the city when the queen allowed her to. Maybe the queen used this vessel to come and go. She had travelled to Glenfel and kidnapped Novia before.

Darius gasped when he and Azura breached the surface. Cold air stung his face.

The ship didn't look much bigger up close — it appeared much smaller than the average trading vessel. *The Bounty* was scratched into one side of it.

"Bones? Jinx?" Azura called out. "Dahlia?" Keeping hold of him, she sprang out of the water, using magic to propel herself.

They landed on the deck with a thud.

Darius wished he had his magic, or at least his senses, to warn him of what he might be up against. Without his magic and in his weakened state, he wouldn't be able to defend himself well.

A dark-haired woman with pale skin came out on deck. "Az, there you are. Where have you been?" She leaned down to get a better look at him. "Who have you got with you?"

"He fell in the river and he's a newcomer here. He is a druid that came through the shield."

"He's not the only one. I ran into a couple myself. Two mind whisperers."

Mind whisperers. That had to be Nyx or her sisters. If they were close by, perhaps he could call them for help.

An ebony-skinned muscular man joined the woman. "What did you bring for us, little sister?" He yanked Darius off the deck. Darius winced from the man's incredible strength. The man's dark eyes narrowed. "He's a dark sorcerer. Look at the dark magic he's covered in. Az, you should just drown him before —"

"No, wait. Look at him." The dark-haired woman held out her hand to stop him. "He's the spitting image of the Archdruid."

Darius opened his mouth to protest, then hesitated. What could he say to get them on his side? Or convince them not to kill him?

"I'm not just a sorcerer, I'm a druid."

Light glowed all over Azura as she shifted into human form and rose to her feet. A long-sleeved tunic, black trousers and boots now covered her. "Maybe we should ransom him back to the Archdruid."

Holy spirits, he couldn't risk being taken back into his father's custody. There would be no chance to escape then.

"My father will never pay to get me back," Darius said. "If you release me, I can help you get through the shield."

"You're the Archdruid's son?" The dark-haired woman narrowed her eyes.

It took him a moment to recognise what she was. Pointed ears, iridescent eyes and a cold energy about her.

An Ilari. Death fae.

His father liked to capture and control them. They were the deadliest of all magickind.

"Then we should just get rid of you." The death fae raised her hand.

"Wait, the queen's gone. None of you will be able to get through the shield without help."

"No one could defeat the queen." Azura scoffed. "That's impossible. Even the Archdruid couldn't defeat her."

"She's gone. I helped defeat her. If you want your freedom, you'll need my help to get out here. Think about it. Stop. I'm more valuable to you if you keep me alive. Do you want to get out?"

Azura tapped her chin. "We'll see if you are as valuable as you say you are."

CHAPTER 13

Nyx's heart pounded in her ears. She, her sisters and the dragons had been searching all around the abandoned buildings close to the palace and the old guard tower. So far, they had found nothing. Except for a couple more dragons. Sirin soon got them in line.

How could Darius disappear? They were linked. She should feel his presence. Why couldn't she? What had gone wrong?

"Where is he?" She paced up and down. "He must be somewhere." Leaves crunched under her feet and she thought she caught faces staring out from the trees a few times.

Dryads, no doubt. She was in no mood to chat with them.

Sirin stood close by, watching her. *I can't sense him. Perhaps he didn't come through,* Sirin remarked. *The shield* —

"The shield doesn't stop me from sensing him. We are —"

What? Linked yes. And more than friends, but she didn't know what that made them. Not lovers either. "He came through. I felt…pain. Then nothing." She turned her attention to the trees. "Do any of you know where he is?"

Fear washed over her like cold water. They knew what she and her sisters were. They knew what the queen was capable of. The trees all fell silent as the dryads retreated back inside them.

"Do you want me to force them out?" Niamh sat perched on a branch. "Maybe he is —"

"Don't say dead. I would know if he was."

"I was going to say injured."

"What are you going to do with the other dragons?" Novia trudged over and several dragons trailed behind her. "Some of them are in a bad way. They show awful signs of mistreatment."

She pushed her hair off her face. The dragons were their responsibility now. They had brought them through. Besides, they couldn't let the poor things be killed off. "Do what you can for them. But finding Darius is our priority." Nyx resumed pacing.

"Shouldn't our main priority be making sure we have food and water?" Niamh jumped down from the branch. "We are stuck here until we figure out how to get through the shield again. We have to survive, don't we?"

She rubbed her temples. Why did everyone keep looking to her for answers? Because Darius was gone. He led everyone. She just stood by him. That didn't mean she knew how to lead people. She would just have to do the best she could. More than anything, she just wanted to find her druid.

Nyx searched her mind for other ways to find Darius. Maybe a spell would help. She chanted a summoning spell and waited. Wind blew around them.

"You think a spell will work?" Niamh arched an eyebrow.

"Anything is worth a try. Go keep looking."

"What about food and more water?" Niamh wanted to know. "We can't trudge to the river every day."

Nyx sighed. "There's a forest here. We should be able to hunt and get things from there. There must be water somewhere near the palace."

"The river isn't far, but a well would be better."

"We've got the queen locked up in that."

"There must be another one somewhere. I'll call Ada and ask her to look."

If she knew the brownie, Ada would already be cleaning more rooms out for them. So she called Ada with her mind.

Ada insisted she'd take care of everything.

"Novia, take the other dragons back to the palace. You can find somewhere to house them there."

"Come." Novia motioned to the dragons, then blurred away in a flash of light.

"Let's keep searching. We'll find him." Niamh squeezed her shoulder.

"I can't understand why he hasn't called me. What if something happened to him?"

"I'm sure it would take more than a fall to harm the Archdruid's son. He could have used his powers to protect himself."

"What if he couldn't? His parents wouldn't let him run away without being able to track him." She pushed further through the trees. *Sirin, Ember, go fly around and see what else you can find.*

Nyx chanted spells as she went. Spells to summon and track.

Nothing worked.

"Damn it, he must be somewhere." Her hands clenched into fists.

"Too bad you're not bound to each other," Niamh muttered.

"Bound?" She furrowed her brow.

"You know, like a soul bond. I couldn't imagine being bound to someone in life and death, though. Nothing lasts that long."

"It doesn't sound so bad if you find someone you love." If they were bonded, at least she would be able to find Darius, no matter where he was.

"Do you love him?"

"I… I don't know." She didn't want to admit how she felt. Every time she thought about not seeing Darius again, pain stabbed through her chest like a knife to her heart. If she did, it would only hurt even more if she lost him.

In what world could they really be together? They'd always had to keep their relationship secret. They couldn't stay trapped here forever. Sooner or later, something would part them. Ambrose had said that, and she feared he was right. Mind whisperers didn't marry for love either. She couldn't be sure her power wouldn't enslave him if they were together.

"Yes, you do. I can see it in your eyes. You love him. Plus, I already know he loves you."

Her mouth fell open. "What? How?"

"He admitted it."

"When? Why haven't you mentioned that before now?" She put her hands on her hips.

She couldn't believe Darius would tell Niamh such a thing. If he did have feelings like that for her, he would tell her. Or at least she thought he would. They had never talked about their feelings very much. If they had, she knew they both feared what might happen. Their relationship was too uncertain to admit anything to each other.

"When the queen took you."

"What were his exact words?"

Niamh frowned. "I don't remember what we said exactly. We were arguing about something and I said, 'but you love Nyx.' And he said, 'of course I do.'"

"That doesn't mean he's in love with me. He could just

love me as a friend. We are good friends." But they had stopped being that a while ago. Now they were stuck somewhere between love and friendship.

If she didn't get him back, she might never know if they could be anything more.

"But you're lovers. You sleep —"

She shook her head. "We aren't lovers. I'm not sure we ever will be."

"Why not? You share the same bed. I find it hard to believe you won't become lovers sooner or later. What are you so afraid of?"

Nyx blew out a breath. "Because it can't work between us. We both know that. Besides, if we become lovers, what if my power enslaved him? Don't you know what happens to people who sleep with mind whisperers?"

"I don't believe the two of you aren't meant to be together. And yes, I know what happens to people who sleep with mind whisperers, but he is immune to your powers. So I don't see why that would be an issue."

"Be realistic. He's the Archdruid's son. And I'm still his enemy. One way or another, something will eventually tear us apart." She looked away. "Maybe it already has. I always knew this would happen — I just didn't know it would be like this."

"Things are different now. He's a rogue. What's stopping you from being together now?"

"That doesn't change anything. Maybe it's better not to fall in love."

"It's a bit late for that." Niamh rolled her eyes.

Arrows whizzed towards their heads. Odd, she hadn't sensed anyone nearby. Her powers must be weaker than she'd expected.

Nyx raised her hand, and the arrows fell to the ground.

"Where did those come from?" Niamh pulled out her

knives.

Nyx scanned the forest with her mind. Minds buzzed nearby. Several of them. *Niamh —*

I sense them too. Who are they?

I guess more escaped prisoners or more likely their descendants. Let's go and find out what they know. One of them might have seen Darius.

You want to find them? Niamh's mouth fell open.

My druid is missing. If they've done something to him, I want to know about it. Let's go. She sprinted off.

Baron, I need you! Niamh called and ran to keep up with her.

Tree branches thwacked against them as they went. More arrows shot in their direction, zipping through the air.

Let's go higher so we can get a good vantage point. She grabbed Niamh's arm and then vanished in a swirl of green orbs. They reappeared on a tree branch.

Now what? Niamh asked.

We wait until they're close enough and we use our powers on them. At least then we can find out everything they know.

The three men came closer. One was a blond elf with long hair and pointed ears, dressed in a long-sleeved green tunic and hose. He had a bow and quiver of arrows. One was a troll that towered above the other two with brownish skin and wore a loincloth. He brandished a large wooden club. The other one had to be some kind of fae, judging by his ears. Long black hair fell past his shoulders and he wore a black tunic, leather jerkin, and hose.

Nyx scanned their minds. *They are Outsiders — whatever that means. I think they are the queen's former prisoners — there are some traces of her in their minds, but I don't think they have had any recent contact with her. They're wondering why we're here.*

Time to have some fun. Niamh smirked. *We should be careful of the troll. They can be hard to take down because of their strength. It's been awhile since I've had the pleasure of playing with one of them.*

Don't kill them. We're here to get answers, not to play with them. Nyx knew just because Niamh wasn't an assassin anymore didn't mean she didn't enjoy a good fight.

I don't kill everyone I meet. Niamh's knives glowed with light as she traced runes over them, then threw them straight at the fae. The knives embedded in his tunic and pinned him to the tree.

"Finiúnacha." Nyx waved her hand and said the druid word for vines. She poured her power into the vines to ensure they would be much stronger and hold their victims in place.

Vines rose and twisted around the elf and troll, pinning them against the other trees. All three men cried out an alarm.

Niamh tried chanting the word too. Vines swirled and wrapped around the fae. "Nice. I need to learn more druid magic."

Nyx scanned their minds further for any trace of Darius and gritted her teeth. "I'm not getting anything from them. Curse it, why don't they know anything? Someone must have seen him!"

"Calm down, sister. We could find out more if we used our touch on them. Mind-reading isn't always accurate. Sometimes people can confuse us with their thoughts."

True enough. She'd met people like that. If someone had a skilled enough mind, they could make their thoughts difficult to read or even create fake images. But she didn't want to waste her energy using her touch unless she had to.

"Let's chat." Orbs of green lights sparkled around them again. They reappeared on the ground.

"What did you do to us?" the elf demanded. "Let us go and or we'll —"

"What? You're tied to a tree." Niamh put a hand on her hip. *That death fae went and told them about us. Damn her. I should have —*

Leave the death fae alone. It would be better if we stayed away from her.

How do you know she doesn't have your druid?

Death fae are known for killing people, not holding them captive.

"Have you three seen a druid around? Tall, blond, too damn good-looking for his own good?" Nyx asked. "Think hard. Or we will use our powers on you."

"Let us out of here," the elf demanded. "You girls have no idea who you are dealing with."

Niamh snorted. "Neither do you. An elf, troll and a fae. You're like the start of a bad joke." She yanked one of her knives out and held it up to the man's throat. "Start talking or I'll start using these on you."

"We know nothing about a druid," the troll snapped. "Who are you two? Ain't seen you before."

Her patience grew thin. Nyx raised her hand and let go of her power. Energy shook the air like thunder without sound. The trees trembled and leaves shot in all directions.

"You will tell the truth now. Where is my druid? He's tall, blond. Has strange markings on his skin."

If Darius had been injured or weakened, he might not be able to glamour his tattoos anymore.

She scanned their minds deeper. "He fell from the sky with the dragons. Someone must've seen him."

"We saw the dragons. They fell through the wall of light," the elf said. "Didn't see no druid."

Niamh squeezed her sister's shoulder. *They know nothing. We'd see it if they did.*

Nyx turned her attention to the trees. "Come out. If you know what we are, you know what we can do." She waited, but no one appeared from the trees.

Dryads saw and heard everything. They were the best way of getting news in any forest. She knew that from experience.

"Or we could just set your trees on fire?" Niamh suggested.

Don't, threatening dryads is a bad idea. Nyx gave her a shove. *We can't afford to make enemies with them.*

I wasn't being serious. Sometimes you have to make a threat or two to get some answers.

I'd rather not make an enemy of everyone in the old city. We are going to need allies sooner or later.

You already threatened them.

She blew out a breath. Niamh had a point. "I'm sorry. I didn't mean to threaten you. I just need… To find my druid. Have you seen anything? We mean you no harm." She glared at the Outsiders. "I can't say the same for you since you already attacked us."

One dryad with bark-like skin, glowing green eyes and long dark hair poked her head out of an oak tree. "We haven't seen anyone."

"She's telling the truth. Come on, let's keep looking. He has to be around here somewhere."

"Then where is he?" She fought back tears. "Someone in this city must know something." Lightning shot from her hand and blew up a tree near them.

The captured Outsiders yelped in alarm.

Niamh's mouth fell open. "How did you do that?"

Nyx stared at her hands as they sizzled with lightning. "I don't know. This isn't my power."

CHAPTER 14

Darius had been fascinated when the ship descended beneath the waves. No ship he'd ever been on had been able to do that before. Most ships travelled by land, air, or both. It seemed to be powered by some kind of crystal magic.

Azura and her crew kept arguing over what to do with him. His limbs were like heavy weights and his blood turned to ice. Azura and her crew seemed unaffected by the cold.

It had taken him a while to figure out who and what they were. Azura, a mermaid. Dahlia, an Ilari death fae. Bones, a gargoyle. There was a fourth member of the crew. Some kind of sprite with gossamer wings, pointed ears, and purple hair, named Jinx.

They made an odd bunch. Darius guessed they must have been brought into the old city by the queen. That was how she got around.

They had given him some water and gruel, at least. But it did little to restore his strength. He needed to get his powers back, and fast. Where had his magic gone? To his father? Or back into Erthea itself, where all druid magic came from? Not all of his power came from nature, so he couldn't be sure.

They had locked him up in an empty cabin with a small bunk to sleep on. But he could still hear them talking from the other room. Darius edged closer to the door and peered through the crack so he could get a good look at the crew.

"What are we going to do with him?" Azura remarked. "He's too valuable to just toss aside. And you know I don't like killing people."

"I think we should ransom him back to the Archdruid once he gets us out of the city." Bones leaned back in his seat.

A glowing orb of light appeared as Jinx, the sprite, materialised. "The druid is telling the truth. The queen's trapped inside a disused well near the old palace." Jinx landed on Azura's shoulder. "There's a barrier of energy keeping her in."

"What about my mother?" Azura furrowed her brow.

Darius leaned closer to the crack in the door.

Mother? What did that mean? Had the queen taken or hurt someone else?

"Her body is there. The queen alternates between sleeping in Lyra's body and wandering about in spirit form," Jinx replied. "She can't leave the well. I think that druid and those newcomers trapped her there. The barrier of energy prevents her from leaving. It's incredible. I never thought anyone would be able to imprison the queen."

Lyra. That had to be Azura's mother. That explained why Azura could shift from mermaid to human form so easily. But how could Azura be Lyra's daughter when the queen had possessed the former priestess for over a century? Azura didn't look old enough. She appeared to be in her twenties perhaps, but it was hard to tell with some magickind who could live for centuries.

"That would explain why the queen hasn't been to see us in over a month," Dahlia remarked. "It's because she couldn't. But how could one druid and those three girls trap the queen?"

Azura shrugged. "You've encountered those girls more than once. Are they powerful?"

"They are mind whisperers. Or at least one of them is. They have tried using their powers on me and they have dragons to protect them."

Bones scoffed. "How could dragons have got through the shield? That thing has been repelling them for as long as I can remember."

"Those mind whisperers must have brought them through." Azura rose from her seat. "I need to get to my mother."

"That's a bad idea." Jinx flitted onto the table. "We can't risk the queen getting loose again. Or we'll be right back to being her prisoners."

"This is my mother we're talking about," Azura snapped. "I've been waiting over ten years to free her from that bloody queen."

"The queen still has her." Dahlia took her hand and squeezed it. "If we rush in to save her, we might set her free again."

"What about the newcomers?" Bones arched an eyebrow. "Can we trust them?"

Dahlia scoffed. "Of course not. They will enslave us just like the queen did."

"But who are they? Why did they come here?" Bones sipped something from a large tankard. "Only Ambrose and the queen can pass through the shield."

"I haven't seen Ambrose either. He hasn't responded to any of our calls." Azura blew out a breath. "The druid might be our only way out."

"Those mind whisperers have Ambrose's staff," Jinx told them.

"They must have done something to him. See, I told you we couldn't trust them." Dahlia's fists were clenched. "I should have used my power against them."

"What if they're immune to your abilities like the queen is?" Bones asked. "I think we need to learn more about them. Find out if they could be a potential ally or not."

Dahlia scowled. "I say we get rid of them. If they hurt Ambrose, they deserve —"

Darius moved away from the door. He needed to get out of here. If these rogues tried to get to Lyra, they might set the queen free.

They faced a big enough threat from his father coming after them. If the queen got loose, there was no telling what she might do. The queen wanted revenge against the Archdruid and she would stop at nothing to get it.

Bones had given him a shirt and boots, but it fell loose over him and the boots were far too big. How could he get out of here without magic? He couldn't swim — they were down far too deep for that.

An air bubble had been conjured around the ship. That was how they breathed and survived down here. Darius doubted all of them would need it. Most of the crew wouldn't be affected by the water or the cold.

Think. How could he get off the ship, back to the surface without magic?

Calling for Nyx, Sirin and the others hadn't worked so far. The only real magic he had left were those strange runes Nyx had etched on him.

His father had said they were old fae magic — protection runes. They were what had kept him alive so far. Could he use them somehow?

Darius tugged the shirt off and ran his fingers over the runes and sigils. Tattoos covered his arms and torso, representing both druid and spirit magic. Odd. None of them had vanished. Did that mean he still had some power left? Maybe his druid magic might be gone, but he had sorcery.

He pricked his finger on a nail he found protruding from a loose board. Blood magic was the most powerful of all. He despised using it, but he had to find some way to reach Nyx. Or everything they had done to stop the queen would be worthless.

He chanted a spell to summon a spirit. *"Spiritus, veni coram me."*

It risked Azura and her crew sensing it, but he had to do something.

Light flared around him, but no spirits appeared.

"That druid is using magic," Azura said.

Good, that meant he did have some power left.

So he tried the only thing he could think of. A spell to stop his heart.

"Nolite cor meum." Darius slumped to the floor and prayed to the spirits this would work.

The door burst open as Azura rushed in.

Darius' spirit appeared, standing over his body.

"Holy spirits, what did he do?" Azura knelt beside him and touched the side of his neck.

Odd. Few people outside of the druids used that curse term.

Were there druids in the old city? Aside from the one Azura had mentioned?

"Curses, he's dead!" Azura gasped.

Dahlia and the others came in after her, looking around in confusion.

"How can he be dead? There's nothing in here he could kill himself with." Bones furrowed his brow.

"I smell blood magic." Dahlia picked up Darius where the blood dripped from his finger.

"I thought you said he was powerless?" Jinx landed and walked across Darius' chest.

"Now how will we get through the shield?" Azura clenched her fists.

Darius knew he had to get out of there before the spell wore off. Which wouldn't be long. His body could only stay dead for a few minutes before his death became permanent.

"Don't be so dramatic." Dahlia knelt beside his body and blew white smoke into his mouth.

Oh spirits, the legend about the Ilari bringing the dead back to life had to be true.

I'm not going back!

Light flashed around him as he reappeared on the deck. He winced as energy pulled at him, tugging him back towards his body.

He pushed back. *Nyx, where are you?* That didn't yield any response.

Instead, he whistled for his dragon. "Come on, Sirin. Come to me."

Darius gasped as his eyes flew open.

"Didn't think you'd escape so easily, did you?" Dahlia gave him a smack, and he knew there'd be no escaping.

CHAPTER 15

Niamh woke to the sound of screaming. She jolted upright. "What now?"

"Novia, calm down. You're safe." Nyx held up her bandaged hands.

"Why am I shackled?" Novia tugged the chain and cursed, glaring at Niamh. "Did you do this?"

"I didn't have much choice. You were going to set the queen free."

"What? I would never do that!"

"We caught you by the well last night." Nyx ran a hand through her hair. "You said you had to free your mistress."

"I'd never release that woman!" Novia cried. "I despise her. You've no idea what she put me through!"

Do you think she is free from the queen's control? Niamh asked in thought. *Or is she pretending?*

Nyx shrugged. *Maybe it's easier to reach her when she's asleep. Free or not, we're not letting her loose again.*

"Please, you know I'd never —" Novia protested.

"We know you don't want to help her, but the queen controlled you. We can't let you go to her." Nyx laid out a tray of food on the bed.

"You can't keep me locked up, either. Please, I can't stay in here. I'll go mad." Tears filled Novia's eyes.

We can't lock her up. She is traumatised by what the queen did, Nyx said.

So we just let her loose? Niamh shook her head. *She will let the queen out.*

Perhaps we can confine her to the palace. We can't watch her all the time.

It's too bad our powers won't work on her. It would be so much easier if we could compel Novia not to go near the queen.

"Fine, we'll confine you to the palace. Andre, you'd better watch her. But if she tries to get near that queen, knock her down." Niamh unhooked the shackle.

"I can't stay here. Who will take care of the dragons?" Novia rubbed her wrist.

"You can. But you are not to go beyond the courtyard." Niamh fumbled in her pack. "I hoped I wouldn't have to use these for a while." She pulled out three crystals.

"What are they?" Nyx frowned.

"Barrier crystals. I'll put them around the courtyard so Novia can't leave. Hopefully, they'll hold her majesty too but we need a plan to deal with her" — she inclined her head to Novia — "and the queen. Staying here is becoming too dangerous. We can't protect the whole palace between the two of us."

"Three," Novia corrected. "I say we go to Glenfel. We can —"

"The minute we set foot outside the shield, what's to stop the Archdruid's magic from following us? Glenfel is his domain. We wouldn't be protected from him there." Niamh arched an eyebrow.

Novia's shoulders slumped. "Maybe I should go there. I wouldn't put anyone in danger if I left."

"That's what Queenie wants, no doubt. We are not splitting up either." Niamh shook her head and turned to Nyx. "We tried staying here. Maybe it's time to face the fact we need to keep moving. To stay one step ahead of the Archdruid."

Nyx's mouth fell open. "No, Andovia is our home. We —"

"This place hasn't been much of a home to me or Novia. If we can't fight off the Archdruid or keep the queen secure, we have to go."

"And what? Keep running?" Novia demanded.

"There's no refuge for mind whisperers in this realm. We're the Archdruid's enemy." Niamh held up a hand when Nyx opened her mouth to protest. "I know you love Darius, but he wanted you to be safe. That's why he forced you to leave."

"I'm not leaving. Not when Darius and Ambrose —"

"Ambrose might as well be dead. Why should we risk ourselves for him? He never even told us who we are." Her hands balled into fists.

"I can't leave and I won't. So forget about it." Nyx swiped the tray onto the floor. Its contents smashed into a pool of water and food. She stormed off without saying another word.

Niamh ran a hand through her hair. "I hate being the bad sister."

"You're not bad." Novia clutched her nose. "Did you hit me?"

"It was either that you would have let Queenie out."

"You're right."

Niamh gaped at her. "What?"

"I said, you're right." Novia sniffed. "Glenfel is my home, or was. But you're both my family and I'll stay with you. No matter what." She grabbed Niamh's hand. "Just promise me you won't let the queen do anything to me. I'm not strong like you."

Niamh wrapped her arms around her. "You can be as strong as you need to be, little sister. I promise that queen will die before she hurts my family."

Novia clung to her. "What are we going to do about Nyx? If she won't leave —"

"She'll come around. Deep down, she knows we're right. Once Ember comes back, we'll plan our escape."

After having breakfast with Novia, Niamh headed to the courtyard and set down crystals. Each crystal hummed and flashed with light. At least it would prevent Novia from leaving. She placed one by the well and marked it to make sure no one could tap into its energy.

They had no idea what the queen was capable of, and Niamh wanted to be careful. Nor did she want to talk to the old harpy but she had to. Just because that witch gave birth to them didn't make her their mother.

Taking a deep breath, she drew magic and willed herself into the well. That took energy — fatigue still weighed on her — but it was the only way to talk to the queen.

She reappeared in the gloom of the well. Her heart thudded in her ears despite being in spirit form.

Lyra's body lay slumped against the wall. Her face was hollow and skeletal.

"Come on, Mother. I know you are awake." Niamh crossed her arms. She spat out the word 'mother'.

Light shot from Lyra's body as the queen's spirit appeared. "I didn't expect you to come and see me. You always were —"

"You need to stay away from my sisters. Novia is not going to release you. None of us will."

Evony laughed. "I won't be stuck down here much longer. How do you really think you can contain me? I'm immortal. You and your sisters aren't."

"You're still trapped in that husk." She scoffed and motioned towards Lyra's body.

Niamh's mind raced. She knew how to force people to talk. But her touch would be useless against the queen. Plus, how could she break someone like Evony?

She had to do something. No way would she let Evony hurt her sisters. "You said something to Nyx about a book. What is it? Where is it?"

Evony scoffed. "I'll tell you nothing. Your sisters were always more obedient than you."

She snorted. "I'm not like them. How do we control the shield?"

Evony said nothing and closed her eyes.

Niamh's form flickered.

"Do you want the Archdruid to come storming into your city again? I mean, Andovia is his now. Your city is ruined and has escaped prisoners running around." Niamh put her hands on her hips. "Don't think you can possess me or compel either. I'm not Novia."

Training with the Order of Blood had been gruelling, but she survived it. One way or another, she would get answers on how to help her sisters.

"I'll get you a new body if you answer my questions."

Evony's eyes opened again. "You'll do no such thing. I know you better than that."

"You want to be more comfortable and I want answers. Let's help each other out. So start talking."

Maybe she could grab one of the Outsiders and use them to get what she needed. She wouldn't let them get possessed — she would just use one of them long enough to get answers.

"Get me a new body then —"

"No one is getting you anything." Nyx's voice echoed from above.

Niamh gasped as she reappeared back in her body.

"What are you doing?" Nyx glared at her.

115

"Trying to get some answers."

"She'll never tell us anything. Don't talk to her. She already used Novia. She will use you too if you let her."

"I'd never let her control me."

"She will use any weakness she can find. So stay away from her," Nyx snapped.

"I had to do something. If we have to stay here —"

Nyx's glower crumpled. "We don't. If it comes to it, I'll leave. But I'm not going to stop looking for Darius."

CHAPTER 16

A few days later, Nyx's heart sank after she and Sirin finished searching another part of the city. "Maybe my sisters are right. Maybe he's not here." She blew out a breath.

He has to be somewhere. We would both know if he were dead, Sirin said.

"Then where is he?" Lightning shot from her hand. The bolt of energy struck the ground with a loud boom.

You need to stay calm.

"I swear if someone says that again, I'll —" More lightning crackled between her fingers. "Why won't this stop? How do I send his powers back to him?"

I can't answer that.

She missed Ember and thought her dragon should be back by now.

Had Ember found the others? Had he got any news? Maybe he couldn't go back through the shield on his own.

That last part seemed unlikely since they knew the shield had weakened. It would come down sooner or later. It still refused to let them pass through it. She and her sisters still hadn't recovered from sending Ember through. They couldn't afford to become weak again. She couldn't go after Ember either.

117

The only good thing that had happened over the past few days was most of her cuts had healed. And they had managed to keep Novia away from the queen.

"Niamh said we'll have to leave soon." Her wings drooped. "I know she's right but —"

You can't leave. Sirin's amber eyes flashed. *We have to find Darius.*

"Do you think I want to leave?" She shook her head. "We can't risk the Archdruid getting the queen." Darius would tell her to leave if he were here. That didn't make it any less painful.

She'd always known they would be torn apart. It made her wish she'd never fallen for him. Never let herself feel anything for him. She tried not to, but there had always been something between them. Something neither of them could ignore.

If you leave, I can't go with you. I have to stay and find Darius.

Pain stabbed through her chest and she nodded. "I know that. And I wouldn't expect anything less." Someone needed to stay here. Leaving would kill her, but she couldn't risk losing her sisters too. "Come on, let's circle around one more time."

They had checked all the buildings on the eastern side of the city. Now was time to check the forest. She'd checked as much as she could from the air. Every time they searched the forest on the ground, the Outsiders attacked.

The time for pleasantries was over. Someone had to know where Darius was.

If he was in the city, someone had him. He would never have gone this long without coming to the palace.

Light exploded overhead and screams rang out. A large black dragon carrying two people appeared.

Dragon Guard? Sirin let out a low growl.

"No, it's Ember." Nyx raised her hands and orbs of green light shot through the sky. The dragon and his two occupants hovered in mid-air. "Ranelle? Lucien? What are you doing here? I thought you couldn't get through."

"Nyx." Ranelle's black, leathery wings popped out, and she flew down to greet Nyx. "We are so glad to see you."

"Your dragon has been telling us everything that happened." Lucien flashed her a grin as Nyx lowered him to the ground.

Darius isn't outside the shield, Ember told her as he landed beside her. *No one on the outside has seen him since the day he disappeared.*

"We wish we could have come his sooner." Ranelle put her hands on Nyx's shoulders. "It took a while to get past the Dragon Guard. But we can't stay outside the old city either."

She clung to Ranelle as tears streamed down her face. "Darius' gone. I can't sense him anymore. What if he…"

"He's not dead." Lucien shook his head. "The Dragon Guard have orders to bring Darius in alive. The Archdruid would know if his son was dead."

She wiped her eyes. "Sorry." Nyx couldn't believe she'd broken down like that. The stress of everything must have got to her.

"Feel free to cry." Ranelle squeezed Nyx's shoulder. "We don't mind."

"We didn't have much luck finding Ambrose," Lucien told her. "We think he is still in the palace, but we couldn't find out much else. Every time we tried to get near, guards blocked our way."

Ranelle nodded. "We didn't dare risk going into the palace. Not with the Dragon Guards looking for us. I'm not sure why the Archdruid thinks we could tell him anything useful. He probably already knows the queen is somewhere in the old city."

In the chaos of everything that had happened over the past few days, she'd almost forgotten about Ambrose. After everything that happened, getting him back hadn't seemed as important. Besides, Ambrose would be safe for now. Whilst in the grip of the queen's enchantment, the Archdruid wouldn't be able to harm him. Or at least she hoped he wouldn't.

"As happy as I am to see you both, I can't say this place is much safer. The shield is faltering and we have to flee soon."

"Flee? You can't leave," Ranelle protested.

"I don't have much choice. When the Archdruid comes through, he'll come straight for the queen."

"You really think you can outrun the Archdruid? There's nowhere on Erthea you could hide from him." Lucien scoffed.

"You really have Darius' magic?" Ranelle frowned.

She nodded. "Don't ask me how." She still couldn't explain that, either.

"You said you felt him die?" Lucien added. "Couldn't you sense where he was?"

"Like I said, I can't sense him. He's vanished. Nothing I've tried so far —" Arrows zipped through the air and came straight towards them. Nyx waved her arm, and the arrows rebounded in the direction they had come from.

"Who is shooting at us?" Lucien asked. "The guards don't use arrows."

"It's not them." Nyx raised her arms and transported them out.

They reappeared in the palace. She filled them in on everything that had happened.

"We should worry about you having Darius's powers," Lucien remarked as they sat around one of the dining halls.

Tapestries covered the walls, depicting different battles from Andovia's history. Ten chairs encircled a round table. Nyx sat there with Ranelle, Lucien and her sisters and listened to what they had to tell her. Ada came in and brought them some tea and some bread and cheese to eat. Ranelle and Lucien both gobbled up the food as if they were starving.

"I'm more concerned with finding him," Nyx protested. "I need to get him back. I dread to think what his father will do to him."

Lucien leaned back in his chair. "We both know Darius is destined to become the next Archdruid. You can't possess that power forever or it will destroy you."

Nyx paled. "I don't even know why they came to me."

"Because you're connected. The bond between you runs deep."

"We don't have a bond." She shook her head. "It's just a link that we got from doing a mind sharing."

Doing a mind sharing and exchanging their knowledge and memories with each other had created a strong connection between them. She didn't understand why anyone could think that would create a bond.

"You love him. That connection alone creates a bond between you," Lucien said. "Love is the strongest of all magics — Ambrose used to say that."

Nyx sighed. "That doesn't help me find Darius."

"The link between you and Darius still exists. Or you wouldn't have felt him die. If we can reverse the connection, you should sense him."

"How do I do that?"

"I can help. I learnt a few things from my mentor, Alaric. We'll need to go somewhere we can concentrate."

121

"I've got patrolling to do." Niamh stood up. "Ranelle, can you help with our queen problem?"

"I'll do my best."

"Good, let's get going." Lucien motioned for her to follow.

She led him up to the room where she had discovered a large spell circle. "But —"

"No buts. If you don't return Darius's powers soon, you could both die. This is just as important as finding Darius and keeping the queen secure." Lucien motioned for her to sit down when they reached the spell circle. "How many times have you lost control?"

"A few times. Just with his lightning, but his powers won't hurt me."

"How can you be sure of that?"

"Because… I feel it."

"Sit and concentrate. As an overseer, I should be able to sense Darius."

"You think he's the one you're meant to protect and guide?"

Lucien shrugged as he sat down in front of her. "I can't be sure. Alaric says when the time is right, I'll know. But it could be you."

"Me?" Nyx laughed. "He's the future Archdruid. I'm nothing compared to that."

"You are the firstborn daughter of the Andovian Queen — that alone makes you very powerful. Firstborn fae are always the most powerful. And you are one of the last mind whisperers. That makes you just as special as he is."

"Let's just find my druid." She held out her hands.

"If this is going to work, you need to put aside any doubts you may have. This kind of magic must come from belief. From truth."

Nyx hesitated. "You know how important he is to me."

122

"Do I?" Lucien quirked an eyebrow. "I've been telling Darius for weeks to admit how he feels about you."

"And did he?"

He shook his head. "Like you, I think he's afraid to."

She understood that feeling well enough. How could she admit how she felt? She couldn't be sure of herself.

Lucien closed his eyes, and her skin prickled as his senses roamed over her. His eyes opened in surprise. "Good gods."

"What? What do you sense?" Her heart pounded in her ears.

"You do have a bond with Darius. A soul bond. Have you shared blood?"

"Of course not. We only did a mind sharing. That wouldn't create a soul bond."

"What about saying the joining vows? You don't need a marriage ceremony to do that."

Nyx shook her head. "I haven't said vows or shared blood with him. We shared power a couple of times, but that's all."

"You are a couple. Since you shared power —"

"We're not a couple. At least we haven't been together in the way you think." Her cheeks flushed.

"Why not?"

Her cheeks burned hotter. "Because — that's not your business." She gave him a shove and couldn't believe he'd asked her such a thing.

"I'm trying to understand how this could happen. His powers must have passed you because of your bond."

Nyx scoffed. "We don't have a soul bond. I can't even find him." She knew the stories of soul bonds. They were rare. If a couple did have one, they were supposed to be able to sense each other no matter how far apart they were.

"That's because you're not letting yourself."

She gaped at him. "That makes no sense. I want to find him more than anything."

"You need to let yourself feel the connection. Only then will you find him."

"I am not feeling it!" Nyx threw her hands up in exasperation. "I can't find him anymore. That's the problem. Don't you think I've tried?"

"I'm just telling you what I sense, Nyx."

"What about his powers? Are they going to kill me or not?"

"You don't have all of his power. I only sensed druid magic, along with your magic. I'd say you're safe. For now."

"How do I feel this connection, then?"

"Only you can do that. Find out what is holding you back."

CHAPTER 17

"Last night, Nyx said she thinks we should talk to the Outsiders. Try to befriend them." Niamh rolled her eyes as she and Novia flew over the forest on Baron and Andre.

"Isn't it better to make friends than have enemies?" Novia and Andre flew alongside her.

Below them, a blanket of green and orange shimmered as the sun rose over the horizon, sending splinters of light across the blue and pink morning sky.

"Maybe, but how can we be friends with a bunch of outlaws?"

"We don't know they're outlaws. And they know this place better than we do." Novia glanced over at Baron. "You're riding him."

"It took you long enough to notice that."

"No, I meant you said you didn't want him."

"Well, he's mine now. He's not so bad." At least Baron didn't chatter all the time. He seemed to understand her own ways her sisters couldn't. "Maybe we should grab one of the Outsiders and get more out of them."

"That wouldn't be a good way to earn their trust." Novia shook her head.

Arrows flew towards them.

"Guess we didn't have to search very far." Niamh raised her hand. *"Srovonadh."*

Light flashed, and the arrows fell to the ground.

"You're using druid magic."

"Nyx taught me a few words and I'm a fast learner. Let's go and see who fired them." Niamh tapped Baron on the neck to signal him to go down.

Baron descended and swooped low over the trees.

Niamh cast her senses out and a cold feeling washed over her. *The death fae is close. I can sense her. Baron, get her.* Niamh winced as branches whacked against her. *We need to work on flying through trees!*

Baron pounced on the death fae and knocked her to the ground.

"What in the blazing hells are you doing?" The Ilari demanded. "Why is this thing on me again? Do you have a death wish, Blondie?"

"Blondie?" She snorted. "And no, I don't. Why are you shooting arrows at us?"

"Do I look like I have anything to fire arrows with?" The Ilari scowled and struggled underneath Baron's enormous mass. "If I wanted to kill someone, I don't need weapons to do it."

She had a point there. It didn't seem likely the death fae had fired arrows. But that didn't make her trustworthy.

"Baron, let her go." Niamh waved her hand as the dragon moved back and she spun a web of energy around the death fae.

The death fae scrambled up and glowered at them. She pushed against the glowing wall of gold energy as it flashed with light. "What do you two want now? Do you make a habit of going around and annoying every person you find in this forest?"

"If you didn't shoot at us, who did?" Niamh put her hands on her hips.

"The Outsiders, no doubt."

"I don't sense any other minds nearby," Novia remarked. "Unless they have shields like she does. Where is the Outsiders' camp?"

The Ilari snorted and scrambled to her feet. "Why would I tell you that? Are you going to harass them now as well?"

Niamh sighed, reached through the web and grasped the woman's throat. Thunder without sound shook the air. The web shattered. Niamh gasped. Her vision went black, and she sank to her knees.

A memory came to her. *She found herself huddled with her sisters, who lay beside her. Blackness surrounded them, she couldn't move.*

Nyx moved and slammed her tiny fists against the solid stone.

Novia lay limp on her other side.

"Niamh? Are you alright?" Novia put her hand on her shoulder and glanced at the death fae. "What did you do to her?"

"I have the touch of death. She should know better than to touch me." The Ilari scowled at them. "You girls must be suicidal." She narrowed her eyes at Niamh. "You saw something, didn't you? Odd, my touch doesn't usually do that to people."

Nyx appeared in a whirl of green orbs. "What's going on? Niamh, I felt you —"

"I'm alright. I — I think I remembered something." Niamh grabbed onto her sisters as they pulled her up.

"I think you need to command her," Novia hissed in her ear. "Give her an order in case your power wears off."

"Take us to the Outsiders." Niamh clung to her sisters for support.

The death fae shook her head. "Find them yourself and stay away from me." She turned and ran off in the opposite direction.

"Let her go," Nyx said. "What did you see?"

"I remember — being trapped somewhere with the two of you. I think we were buried." She grimaced. "What does that mean? Were we dead?"

She knew Nyx kept having nightmares about being buried. But what Niamh had seen had only been a brief glimpse. Nothing like what Nyx experienced.

"I think they buried us after… What happened in the city," Nyx replied. "Being close to death must have triggered it. That's how I remembered you were my sister."

"So being close to death helps us to remember?" Niamh furrowed her brow.

"I wish I could remember more." Novia sighed.

"Maybe we've found a way of getting our memories back," Nyx said.

After searching the forest further, they still had no luck finding the Outsiders' camp. So they headed back to the palace.

"You want to cast a spell to mimic death?" Niamh's mouth fell open.

"Do you know another way of getting our memories back?" Nyx arched an eyebrow. "Besides, Novia took poison once so she could access her memories."

Novia bit her lip. "Niamh has a point. What if something goes wrong?"

"Maybe we should cast a spell." Nyx headed down the hall and shoved open some doors. "I found the circle this morning. So we have somewhere to cast the spell." The room opened up into a large space with bare sandstone walls and a shimmering silver circle on the flagstone floor. Runes.

"I'm not sure about this." Novia wrung her hands together.

Niamh grimaced. "I'm not sure I want to remember being buried alive." That memory frightened her, and she didn't want to experience it again.

"I'll cast the spell then. You two don't have to be part of it." Nyx stepped into the circle and the runes shone brighter.

Niamh's mouth fell open. "And risk you dying? No." She stepped into the circle. "Novia?"

Novia hesitated. "We have to stick together. We're stronger that way." She climbed in after them.

The sisters sat and linked hands.

"Lig dwinn codladh cosulle bas," Nyx chanted in the druid tongue.

Niamh and Novia repeated it with her. Energy reverberated through the circle. Niamh slumped onto her side.

She found herself back inside the darkness. Only this time, it was a room.

Slivers of moonlight shone through the window. The sound of raised voices echoed through the blackness. Niamh turned and around spotted a woman with large wings arguing with a bearded man. Somehow, both figures felt familiar to her.

"Where were you?" the woman demanded. "You've been gone for hours."

"I had business to take care of," the man replied.

Niamh peered closer. Ambrose and the queen — her parents.

Her sisters wriggled in the bed beside her. Even though they had their own beds, they often slept together as they enjoyed being close to each other. Their mother always scolded them about that and said they were too old for such nonsense.

"What business?" the queen hissed. "Tell me where you were."

"The Archdruid's forces followed me. I had to... waylay them. It's late. Let's get some sleep." Ambrose took the queen's arm and led her out of the room.

Once the door closed, all three sisters sprang up from the bed.

Niamh reached the door first. She pressed her ear against it.

"Are they gone?" Nyx grabbed Niamh's hand.

"No, Papa is still there talking to Vel. I can't hear what they're saying."

Novia came over and took Niamh's other hand. All at once, their senses heightened.

"You have to take the girls to the river," Ambrose said. "Get them out of the city. I have a boat waiting for them. Go now."

The sisters glanced at each other, then raced back to their beds as footsteps approached.

Their mother's presence washed over them like fire.

"Ambrose, what are you doing?" the queen demanded.

"Nothing. Just making sure the girls are well protected."

A few moments later, the voices faded, and the door creaked open.

Velestra stood there clad in armour. She stared at them for a few moments, then left.

All three sisters lay there unmoving, barely daring to breathe.

"Why does Papa want us to leave?" Novia whispered.

"Something bad is going to happen." Nyx shivered.

"What?" Niamh clutched the hem of her long white nightgown. "Maybe you should tell Mama."

Novia shuddered. "No. She'll be angry again."

Niamh blinked. Her head pounded as she found herself back in the circle. "What was that?" She groaned.

Nyx and Novia scrambled up. "Another memory. Looks like Ambrose was the one who let the Archdruid in."

CHAPTER 18

"Find out what's holding you back."

Nyx had scoffed at Lucien's words. She wanted to find Darius more than anything. Why would any part of her be holding her back?

She had no doubt she wanted him back. Wanted the connection between them restored. Yet every time she reached for him with her senses, she felt nothing. Lucien said the problem was emotional. Insisted she needed to admit to herself how she felt.

She agreed to stay at the palace that morning whilst Niamh and Lucien searched for Darius and the elusive Outsiders. Maybe finding them would finally lead to some answers. He had to be somewhere in the city. Somehow, she knew he'd come through the shield. Sometimes she thought she felt glimpses of him. But whenever she reached for that feeling, it always disappeared.

She still had got no closer to solving the problem of finding Darius a couple of days later. Ranelle insisted they search the palace further that morning.

"The queen must have a library or some sort of vault around here somewhere. We can find it." Ranelle gave her a determined look as they strolled down the hall on the ground floor.

"That would be good." Nyx yawned and rubbed her aching eyes. Fatigue weighed down on her like a heavy cloak.

"When was the last time you slept?" Ranelle frowned at her.

She waved a hand in dismissal. "I can't sleep. Because… I have too much on my mind."

"And because you miss Darius," Novia added. "I don't understand why you don't just admit how you feel. It's easy."

Nyx scowled at her. "You sound like Niamh."

"Niamh has a point."

"Nyx, you can't keep using magic to force the way your fatigue. That's not healthy," Ranelle chided.

"Until you figure out how you feel, you won't find your druid." Novia crossed her arms and leaned back against the wall.

"That's not true. We have more important things to deal with than me sleeping." Nyx drew magic and forced her tiredness away again. She had been doing that a lot since Darius' disappearance. "Let's focus on finding records. There must be something around here to show us how to control the shield." Nyx tapped the screen to show them a map of the palace. "Should we take a floor each?"

"Wouldn't it be safer to stick together?" Novia asked. "What if that shapeshifter you and Niamh encountered is still here?"

"It's not. I already checked there."

Ranelle grinned as she stared at the screen. "The magic in this palace is beyond anything I've encountered before. I wonder how it works. Using such a large network of crystals must be ancient, advanced magic. I doubt even the Archdruid could do this."

"Let's split up. Call if you need help." Nyx headed up to the third floor. If she were the queen, she imagined this might be where her chambers would be. It had taken a while to get the outer doors to open. Odd, as most of the palace had been wide open.

"Keeper, what was this floor used for?" Nyx glanced around.

The walls gleamed with white paint and gold filigree. The floor shone with white marble.

"I am not permitted on this floor without the queen's permission."

To her surprise, the keeper didn't appear as usual. "Why? I thought you could go everywhere in the palace?"

"Not everywhere. Those are my orders. I cannot defy her."

"Defy her? Are you saying the queen still has control over you somehow?" Nyx moved further down the hall. Suits of armour holding shining swords and spears stood guard. She half expected some of them to come to life.

The keeper didn't answer. That disturbed Nyx.

"Keeper, are you a prisoner here?" She stopped moving, glancing up and down the hall with its rich sandstone walls. The crystal torches that lit up the space flickered.

"Indeed, my lady. I have been trapped within the palace walls for as long as I can remember."

"Wait, do you mean the queen somehow put you inside the crystal system that controls the palace?" Her mouth fell open. "Aren't you a being created out of magic?" She had seen golems and other beings created from magic before. Their sole purpose was to serve their creators. Nyx had thought the keeper was like them.

"No, I don't think I was created from magic. I know I had a life before I became the queen's prisoner. But most of that is a distant memory now. One I can't even remember." The keeper sounded almost sad at that.

Her hands balled into fists. Did her mother enslave everyone she encountered? "That's awful. Is there any way to set you free?"

"No, if you were to free me, I would no longer exist in the physical world. Nor do I want freedom. I am safe within these walls."

Nyx fell silent for a moment. "Can you at least tell me what this floor was used for?"

"I cannot answer. The queen forbade me from telling anyone what's up here."

"You don't have to obey her anymore."

"I cannot disobey her."

"Are you saying you're still communicating with her?"

Again, the keeper didn't answer, so Nyx took that as an affirmation.

Gods, they had to render the queen powerless. Even locked up, she still wreaked havoc on everything.

Only one door lay at the end of the corridor. When she reached for the door handle, something sizzled against her skin. Of course, the queen would put up a barrier.

Gripping the locket she'd found, she let the queen's magic flow freely. Or at least the glimmer of energy that held the image showing them as a family.

After a few seconds, the enormous wooden door swung open. Nyx couldn't make out much of anything in the blackness.

"Lights," she ordered. One thing she'd learnt about the palace was the crystals flared to life when commanded.

Nothing happened.

She raised her hand and conjured a large green orb. Not so much to see by, but to make herself feel more comfortable in the darkness.

A black mass shot towards her. Tendrils of smoke wrapped around her throat. The shadow took the form of a man with a balding head and dark eyes. "Who dares to enter my queen's domain?"

Nyx coughed as he squeezed her throat tighter. What was this thing? She raised her hand, sending out a blast of green orbs. It did nothing to deter her assailant. She guessed by the smoke this had to be some type of spirit. No doubt meant to guard the queen's chambers.

Stop, you fool. I'm the queen's daughter.

He continued choking her. The blade from her bracelet came out and she slashed at him. The sword passed straight through him.

The queen's guardian laughed. "Stupid girl. No weapon can harm me."

She chanted words to a spell to repel the spirit using sorcery. "Invicta spiritus."

An image flashed through her mind. She stood before this spirit and said something to him. A word whispered through her mind.

Nothing. The flash of memory faded as quickly as it had begun.

Get away from me! She let go over all control she had over her power and Darius'. Lightning shot from her hands. The man evaporated.

Nyx gasped for breath and rubbed her throat.

The smoke reformed, and the guardian lunged for her.

Nyx raised her hand, which glowed with light. "I'm the Morrigan's daughter. Stay away from me." A shield of energy formed in front of her. Another part of Darius' magic? She couldn't be sure.

The guardian's lip curled. "The queen's daughters are dead. You're an impostor."

She flipped open the locket, so the hologram reappeared. "Look, that's me." She pointed to the child with wings in the centre.

He shook his head. "Impossible. They all died."

"Well, we came back. So stay away from me." She closed the locket and shoved it back into the pocket of her tunic.

"You have an aura of the Archdruid." The guardian sneered.

She snorted. "I doubt that."

The Guardian held up a hand to stop her. "Only those who know the secret word may pass into the queen's chambers."

Nyx froze. Secret word? How could she learn that?

She scanned the Guardian with her senses. He felt like a spirit, yet not. Something beyond a spirit. No words came to her.

"Willow." That was the only word she could remember. The one she had heard when he had choked her.

"You may pass. But where is my queen? It's unlike her to stay gone for so long."

"She's not coming back."

"What do you mean, Aerin? Where is your mother?"

She shook her head to clear it. "Nothing. The queen is… Indisposed."

"Where is she? She never leaves me alone for so long. If she is injured —"

"She's fine. I wouldn't be here if she wasn't."

"How did you come back?"

"That's not important. Leave me," she snapped.

The Guardian vanished in a whirl of smoke.

Nyx let out a breath she hadn't known she had been holding. She couldn't risk that Guardian finding out about what they had done to the queen. And she had no idea what the name Aerin meant.

Had that been her name?

She hadn't considered her name might be different. Since she had known her name when she'd woken up under an ash tree. Nyx had always been her name. The name Aerin didn't feel like it belonged to her.

Pushing her churning thoughts away, she headed through another set of double doors.

Crystal torches cast shadows around and a giant crystal chandelier flared with light, glittering like diamonds.

Gold filigree covered the walls in the shape of trees. A white fur rug covered the floor and plush divans and high-back chairs stood near a carved hearth. It looked more like a parlour than a bedchamber.

Nyx found another set of double wooden doors and pushed them open.

Another chandelier, dripping with crystals that sparkled like diamonds, hung overhead. Gold covered the walls. The paintings of Andovia and tapestries covered the parts that didn't shine like molten lava. A lake-sized bed stood draped in golden linens.

More doors led off in different directions. One a room with a large bathing pool. Another a wardrobe with filled with clothes.

The queen had mentioned a book. Nyx knew she must have kept her wealth of knowledge somewhere. There wasn't much sign of Ambrose's things. She wondered if Ambrose had separate chambers. That wouldn't surprise her.

Scouring around the queen's chambers revealed little. No sign of a book or anything useful.

Heading into the hall, she found another chamber. This one was much less opulent than the queen's and more masculine. This had to be Ambrose's room. Clothes, books and other items still cluttered the space.

A large green leather-bound book lay on the green fourposter bed. Along with a crystal. Picking the crystal up, she yelped when it flared with heat.

The crystal fell to the floor as a projection of Ambrose appeared. He glanced behind him as if he expected someone to come in.

"Ambrose." She gasped. "How are you here? I thought the —"

"Nyx, if you're seeing this, I know I'm no longer with you. No doubt I have fallen into the hands of the queen or the Archdruid." He stared ahead, like he couldn't see her. "I know you must have questions. Which is why I have left you this message, along with the queen's grimoire. It will help you navigate the city and any problems you might face. Be sure to activate the runes on it so no one but you can touch it. Not even your sisters." Ambrose glanced behind him. "The queen will stop at nothing to get what she wants. Even if it means using your sisters against you."

Nyx scoffed. "She can try."

"If you're forced to stay in the old city, be sure to befriend the Outsiders. They may not be welcoming at first, but I'm sure you and Darius can convince them."

"Forget the Outsiders. Tell me how to control the shield." She knew this had to be a recorded message, but she said it anyway.

"If the leader of the Outsiders won't help you, go to Taliesin. He lives in the forest not far from the Outsiders. Find Azura and her crew. They are good people. They have worked with the resistance too — when the queen wasn't forcing them to do her bidding," Ambrose told her. "Azura keeps company with a gargoyle, a sprite, and an Ilari." His brow creased. "I'm sorry I can't be there. Nyx… There's so much I need to tell you…"

"Telling me you're my father would have been a good place to start. You knew all along." She glowered at him.

"The shield around the city is weakening.... Only the queen can restore it. Her power alone controlled it."

"That doesn't help."

"The queen's vault of knowledge is on this floor. Concealed by torches. Press the torches in sequence three times. The queen's body is hidden —"

The projection faded away.

"Come back. What were you going to tell me?"

Nothing she said or did would make the message play any longer.

CHAPTER 19

"You were a fool to try and escape." Azura wrapped rope around his hands again as she led him on deck. "We won't hurt you."

He scoffed. "You've already talked about killing me."

"I don't kill people."

"That's unusual for Merkind to say, given how much you like to sink ships."

"Not all Merkind drown people or sink ships. I'm different. I could say all druids are bad, given who your father is." Azura finished tying his hands, then wrapped the rope around a post.

"They're not."

"You used blood magic."

"Not all blood magic is evil." Besides, it was the only magic he could use.

"You don't have any power, do you?" Azura arched an eyebrow. "That cuff drained it."

"I have some power." He didn't want them to think he was powerless. Or they were more likely to kill him. He had to figure out another way to escape, or at least get a message to Nyx or Sirin.

He didn't have a strong enough connection with anyone else for them to hear him. The shield would block the connection to anyone outside the old city.

Darius wished he had stronger connections to people. Getting close to others had always been risky. Ranelle and Lucien had worked with Ambrose. Nyx had come to live with the old druid. That was why he had formed connections with them.

Azura scoffed. "There's barely any power left in you. Your father must have taken it. I doubt that makes you much use to me or my crew."

"I can help you get through the shield. If you take me to Taliesin, he can verify I'm not like my father."

"No, you're not the Archdruid, but that doesn't make you an ally."

"I'm not your enemy, either. You can't let the queen out."

"That bitch deserves to die after everything she's put us through. For what she did to Lyra."

"Lyra is important to you." He caught the flash of pain in her eyes. "But you can't save her whilst the queen is still attached to her."

"You don't know that. If the queen's —"

"The queen is still in Lyra's body. They're both trapped."

"You could get the queen out of Lyra. You're covered in symbols of spirit magic."

Darius shook his head. "Even at full power, I can't do that. She's too strong."

"We'll see. Or I can trade you to the mind whisperers or the Archdruid." She finished tying him to the post.

"Will you at least let me try to get you out of the city?"

If he got them outside the shield, the Dragon Guard would attack. He could use the distraction to escape.

The sprite landed on Azura's shoulder. "The shield is under constant attack. No one is getting through it."

"Jinx, go and check on the queen. We'll be ready to attack soon." Azura wandered off. "One way or another, I'm getting my mother out of that well."

Darius struggled against the ropes. He would have to use whatever power he had left. He never used sorcery unless he had to. It brought back too many awful childhood memories of being forced to use magic in a way he never wanted to. But now he needed that power.

He chanted words of power. Nothing. Sorcery never came as easily as druidry.

He tried again.

"Your magic won't work." Bones leaned against the helm.

"I have to try. Please talk some sense into Azura. Letting the queen out won't bring you freedom."

"And why would we listen to a Valeran?" Dahlia came up behind Bones and scowled at him. "You can't imagine what the queen has put us through."

"You've got a chance of freedom; do you really want to throw that away?"

"He has a point," Bones agreed. "Maybe —"

"Don't side with him." Dahlia whacked Bones over the head. "Fool. We don't listen to prisoners."

Bones rubbed the back of his head and winced. "But we've wanted our freedom for decades. You want it. We all do. If we —"

Dahlia glared daggers at him. "If the queen is contained, we can capture her."

Darius scoffed. "You'll never capture her. And you can't kill an immortal." He'd seen his father use death fae before. Immortals couldn't be killed. Only subdued. That was how his father had stayed in power for so long.

Maybe if they took him with them, he could escape.

Jinx reappeared a few moments later as Bones and Dahlia argued over their next move.

"The queen's unguarded, but someone has placed crystal barriers around the well," Jinx told them.

Bones rumbled with laughter. "Crystals won't stop me."

Jinx landed on the helm. "They're filled with strong magic. I saw Elven and other runes on them."

Elven runes. At least Niamh had the sense to keep the queen secure. He hoped the crystals would be enough to keep Azura and her crew out.

"Let's get moving." Azura came back on deck with the sword strapped to her back. "We need to strike whilst those mind whisperers are distracted."

"One of them left the palace on a dragon. Not sure about the others." Jinx flew over and landed on Azura's shoulder. "They might still be there, but they can transport themselves to different places.

"I can handle the mind whisperers. They're not the queen." Dahlia smirked.

"Let's get going." The runes on the helm flared to life as the ship rose off the riverbed. It didn't rise to the surface. Instead, they floated through the churning waves.

The river flowed out of the realm into the sea. From what he'd heard, the shield encompass the river as well. Or else his father would have found a way through long before now.

"You really think you can get near the queen?" Darius frowned at them.

"We've broken out people before. Even on Glenfel — which is supposed to be impenetrable." Azura smiled.

"But you had the queen to help you."

Novia hadn't told them everything about being taken but had said the queen and Ambrose came for her. How the queen managed to get to the island, he could only guess.

Darius had got through when he went there with Nyx because he knew how his father worked. But it had taken months to get the crystal to penetrate the island's defences. It had been a stroke of luck since he'd had it in the first place. He'd only decided to get a crystal in case he ever needed it.

His mind raced. It wouldn't take long to get to the palace. Escaping before then seemed impossible.

When they got closer to the riverbank, all four crew members pushed their way through the bubble. Azura dragged him along with her. He winced as the cold washed over him and gasped when they reach the surface.

"Everyone ready?" Azura asked as they all scrambled onto the bank.

"As I'll ever be." Bones pulled out a pouch and threw sparkling dust over them.

Darius sneezed as the dust tickled his nose. "What's that for?"

"To stop anyone from seeing or sensing us." Bones kept a tight grip on him as they pushed their way through the forest.

Branches snagged at his skin and clothes. Darius chanted spells in his mind. To summon spirits. To call up the wind. Just because the cuff drained his power didn't mean he didn't have some left.

Damned cuff. If he got it off, his magic might work. Azura and her crew hadn't been able to remove it either.

The palace, with its sandstone walls, loomed ahead. His heart skipped a beat. This would be the closest he'd been to Nyx in days. Somehow, he had to find a way to contact her.

Bones kept a tight grip on his arm, and Dahlia stayed on the other side of him. No chance of escaping as they moved away from him.

The courtyard lay ahead. The flagstones broken and burnt in places. Crystals lay situated a few feet from the well.

Azura held up her hands. A wall of energy flickered in front of her. "Bones." She motioned the big man forward.

The gargoyle stepped up beside her. Light flashed around him as he balled his fists and punched against the barrier.

Darius winced. Dahlia gripped his arm. "Don't try anything, druid."

"You won't get through. Those girls aren't stupid."

Bones continued pounding against the barrier, and Jinx hurled bolts of energy at it.

"Azura, hold the druid." Dahlia shoved him towards the mermaid. The death fae walked towards the shield, wincing as it blocked her.

That relieved him. Most barriers didn't repel her kind.

"How do we get through?" Azura demanded.

He shrugged. Magic stirred inside him for the first time since this nightmare started.

Why had it returned now? Had something triggered it? It didn't matter.

Azura gripped his arm and shoved him forward. He stumbled and passed through the barrier.

Azura followed after him, and she grinned. "Told you he would be useful." She reached out to grab Dahlia.

Darius struggled against her grasp. The mermaid drew back and slapped him. His head reeled back. Holy spirits, what would it take to get these people to see sense?

Dahlia, Bones, and Jinx came through next.

Azura kept a firm grip on him. "Why did you put her in a well?"

"It was the only place we could find to trap her. But you can't —"

"Do you want me to strike you again?"

The barrier over the well repelled Azura as she reached out for it. Dahlia reached out too and her hand passed through it.

Holy spirits, why hadn't he thought to keep an Ilari out? He had added runes to stop any spirits passing through, but the magic would have to be designed to repel someone like Dahlia.

"I'll grab her." Dahlia jumped into the well.

Darius drew more power. He'd have to use everything he had to stop them.

Would it be enough?

The symbols on his chest flared with light.

Dahlia jumped back up, dragging Lyra's body with her.

"Holy spirits, what have they done to her?" Azura let go of him and rushed forward.

Lyra's eyes flew open, blazing with light. "Why are you fools here?"

"Let go of my mother," Azura snapped. "You're free. You can leave her now."

The queen laughed. "I'll never release her. But I could use a new host."

Darius raised his hand and started chanting.

The queen growled. "You really think you can take me on, boy?"

He used his free hand to blast Azura and her crew back through the barrier. "Avock!" Darius raised his hands and blasted the queen back into the well. Runes flared with light as he triggered the other protections around the well.

Dahlia fell to the ground, but his power wasn't strong enough to force her out.

"You're not going anywhere." Darius pushed against the queen with his power. Sweat broke out across his brow as he pushed his power against her.

He might not have his druid magic, but he did have sorcery, and very few sorcerers were more powerful than his mother. Her power ran through his veins. He called more magic to him, pushing as the queen's energy pressed down on him like a heavyweight.

The queen laughed. "You've lost your druid magic. That would explain why Nyx has become so much more powerful."

What did that mean? How could Nyx have his power? That made no sense.

She threw an energy ball towards him, striking him in the chest.

Darius sank to his knees, but he refused to falter. "I'm not powerless. Now go!" Energy reverberated through the air and she screamed as she fell back into the trap.

He took a deep breath as his heart slowed. What was happening to him? Had the queen's magic affected him that much?

His vision darkened as he gasped for breath. Darius reappeared standing over his body again.

No. He hadn't come close to death this time. Or at least he didn't think he had.

Why did this keep happening and could he use it to escape?

CHAPTER 20

Novia's stomach churned as she headed up to the third floor. The queen's familiar scent of jasmine sickened her. She closed her eyes and told herself not to think about her imprisonment again.

Andre brushed up beside her and nuzzled her. *The queen can't hurt you.*

"We both know that isn't true." Novia flung open the door to another chamber. According to the keeper, the place contained seven hundred rooms. Twenty state rooms. Thirty bedrooms. Some rooms reminded her of workrooms. They had found one or two rooms with books in and a few records, but no main library.

Why did the queen keep the library locked up? Libraries were supposed to be a place for everyone to enjoy. She and her sisters must have studied somewhere. Novia got the impression the queen would have made sure they were well educated. She had known how to take care of herself and how to read when she went to Glenfel. Things slaves weren't taught. As well as being able to understand a couple of different languages.

Nyx and Novia both knew how to use weapons. Especially swords. Someone had to have taught them. Ophelia always said she had the manners of a highborn lady. She never expected to be a princess.

No, she wouldn't call herself that. The queen had been overthrown a century ago, and Andovia didn't need her back in power.

Novia, I've found something.

She pushed open the double doors. Novia yelped when a man appeared in a whirl of smoke. She put a hand to her chest. "Who are you?"

"Gemmill, the queen's guardian. Who are you?"

"She's my sister. I thought I told you to leave?" Nyx scowled at him.

The man's eyes narrowed. "How are you both alive?"

"That's not your business. Now go!" Nyx crossed her arms.

Gemmill vanished in a whirl of smoke.

"Who's that?"

"He protects this place for the queen. Come on." Nyx motioned for her to follow. "Don't tell him anything about us."

"Why not?"

Because he could still be linked to the queen. Nyx switched to talking in thought. *We can't trust him.*

Novia sat and watched the recording Ambrose had made.

"Here's the grimoire." Nyx held up the book.

"Did you find anything useful in it?"

"There's a lot about the history of mind whisperers in there."

"What about the shield?"

"Nothing so far. But I'm hoping there's something. I will keep looking."

Novia hesitated as she reached for the book and backed away. "Maybe I shouldn't touch it."

Nyx's eyes widened. "Why not?"

"Because the queen can control me. I don't want to risk anything."

"Ambrose says we should befriend the Outsiders."

"And you believe him?"

Nyx shrugged. "I don't see why he'd lie about that."

"How do you know that's not playing into the queen's hands?"

"You said we should —"

She blew out a breath. "Sorry. I can't trust anyone right now. Especially not myself."

"I found something in here that says how to break a mind whisperer's hold. A mind whisperer's touch can be broken — even by compulsion or by choosing to release someone from compulsion. There's something else that says the Morrigan can break any mind whisperer's hold on someone. Or a group of mind whisperers can break the hold." Nyx's eyes flickered over the pages. "Maybe Niamh and I can break her hold on you." She waved her hand so Niamh appeared in a swirl of orbs.

Niamh and Baron crashed onto the floor, screaming as they skidded across the tiles. "Will you please not do that?" Niamh scrambled off her dragon.

"Sorry, but we need you."

"Call first, summon later." Niamh's eyes widened as she glanced around the room. "Now this is lavish."

"It's the queen's chambers." Novia scowled. "It's horrid and tacky."

"The queen might be a witch, but she had good taste." Niamh scrambled off the dragon. "What do you need me for?"

"I found the queen's grimoire," Nyx told her what Ambrose's message had said. "Ambrose said to find someone called Azura and her crew."

"A gargoyle and a sprite were on the ship that took me from Glenfel. That must be who he meant." Novia scowled.

"We can't work with a death fae." Niamh scoffed. "Besides, why should we listen to anything Ambrose says? He's not trustworthy."

"We do need allies in the city. If the shield comes down, the Outsiders deserve to be warned," Nyx pointed out.

"Why?" Niamh frowned. "They keep attacking us."

"That's because they think we're the enemy. Maybe we should talk to them. Let them know we're not a threat," Nyx mused.

"Have you forgotten the part about us leaving? We can't survive in a dead city with our mad mother locked up in a well." Niamh shook her head.

"I say we should stay. At least until we can figure out how to safely move the queen." Nyx tucked the grimoire under her arm. "I also know the entrance to the queen's vault. Let's go and see it. Maybe we can find something useful in there."

The three of them headed out into the hallway. Nyx went up to a set of three crystal torches that hung at the end of the passage. "Ambrose said something about using these in sequence. It is very similar to how the Archdruid accesses his vault." She tapped each of them.

The three of them waited, but nothing happened.

Nyx cursed. "If only Ambrose could have told us how to open it."

"Didn't you say something about how you used your powers to open the Archdruid's vault once with Darius?" Novia asked.

Nyx nodded. "Maybe we should all use our powers." She put the grimoire on the floor and held her hands out for her sisters.

Niamh hesitated. "What if she set a trap for us in there? I wouldn't put anything past that woman."

"We'll be careful." Novia gripped Nyx's hand.

Light flared outside the window on the east side of the room. "What's that?" Novia furrowed her brow. "Has the shield failed?"

"It's a warning. Someone is near the well. Let's go." Nyx grabbed their arms and transported them out.

They reappeared near the well.

Darius lay sprawled on the ground with the Ilari standing over him. A silver-haired woman with a sprite and a huge, dark-skinned man stood nearby.

"They're the ones who kidnapped me." Novia put her hand over her mouth as Nyx let go of her.

"Azura." Niamh gaped at the silver-haired woman. "What are you doing here?"

"You know them?" Novia sneered and Niamh didn't get a chance to answer.

"Darius." Nyx gasped and moved forward. Her sisters grabbed her arms to stop her from going any further. "What have you done to him?"

"And what are you doing here?" Niamh repeated, and palmed one of her knives.

"Stay back or I will kill your druid," the death fae warned. She ran a hand over Darius's unconscious face.

Nyx closed her eyes, her entire body trembling. Light flared around her.

What's going on? Niamh asked. *What is she doing?*

Nyx screamed and energy jolted through her.

I don't know. Novia took a step back.

When Nyx opened her eyes again, they bled to black. Energy radiated from her; fury mixed with power.

Niamh swore under her breath. "That is not good."

Nyx's hand shot out; energy impacted the air like thunder without sound. The force rattled Novia's bones. She and Niamh stumbled backwards.

The four Outsiders screamed, their bodies writhing in agony.

"What's she doing?" Novia gasped.

"She's in the blood rage. We have to stop her!" Niamh threw herself at Nyx, knocking her to the ground.

Blood rage. The words rolled like ice down her spine. Novia knew they meant something terrible. As though something inside her knew what they meant.

"What do we do?" Novia knelt by her struggling sisters as Nyx thrashed against Niamh. "What is it?" Just because the words felt familiar didn't mean she understood what they meant. Other than being something bad.

"It's an uncontrollable force when a mind whisperer becomes controlled by the dark side of their gift." Niamh struggled to get hold of Nyx's arms. "Help me! She will kill them and anyone who gets in her way."

"Maybe we should let her." Novia got hold of Nyx's legs as she continued to thrash and kick. "At least they wouldn't be able to hurt anyone else." Novia never thought she would wish death on anyone. She had spent the last few years surrounded by some of the worst criminals on Erthea. But these people had helped the queen capture her. She didn't think she could forgive them for that.

"A mind whisperer in the blood rage can lose their soul to darkness. She'll become damned if we let her give into it."

Damned.

Novia's blood went cold. She knew the damned well enough. She met one on Glenfel. A woman with an insatiable need for blood. Gods, she couldn't let that happen to her sister.

The Outsiders fell to their knees.

Knock her out like you did with me, Novia suggested. She didn't want to remember the night she had tried helping the queen. Since then, her sisters had done everything they could to make sure she didn't go anywhere near the well.

Niamh swung at their sister. Nyx dodged the blow, raised her hands and sent Novia and Niamh flying with a blast of energy.

Novia gasped as she hit the palace wall. The air left her lungs in a whoosh.

The silver-haired woman raised her hand and light swirled around them. Darius and his captors disappeared in a splash of water.

Nyx shot into the sky, the downdraught from her wings almost knocking her sisters over.

Dragons, get out of here! Niamh yelled and all three dragons appeared in a flash of light. *Ember, go follow her and stop her!*

Ember roared; his massive wings outstretched as he took to the air.

She leapt up and held her hand out for Novia. "Come on, we need to follow her."

Laughter echoed from inside the well. "The blood rage can't be stopped. It's uncontrollable."

"Shut up, Mother," Niamh snapped.

"How are we going to stop her?" Novia clung to Andre as he and Baron took to the air. "I've seen the damned before. There's no coming back from that. Why would she even go into the blood rage?"

"Probably because that Ilari threatened the druid. If we get him back, maybe we can save her."

"Can't we talk to her? How do you even know what the blood rage is?"

Niamh shook her head. "I've been warned about the blood rage since I joined the Order. You can't reason with anyone whilst they are in it. One way or another, we have to bring her out of there before we lose her forever."

CHAPTER 21

Darius gasped for breath as he, Azura, and her crew landed in the river. The mermaid kept a firm grip on his arm.

His wet hair stuck to his face and neck. "Where are we?" Fatigue weighed down on him, heavy and unrelenting. At least he'd forced the queen back into her prison. Maybe he would have seen Nyx if the queen hadn't knocked him down.

"Near the old dock." The mermaid glanced around. "Holy spirits, what did that mind whisperer do to us?"

Dahlia groaned. "Az, couldn't you at least have sent us to the ship?"

"No, those girls might follow us." Bones struggled to stay afloat. "Gods, that girl's touch felt like the queen's power."

"What are those girls to you?" Azura glared at Darius.

"The one who attacked you is my life, mate. I warned you not to go near the queen."

How had the queen's power not touched him? Maybe Nyx's magic had somehow kept him alive. He reached out to Nyx with his mind again. Something tingled at the edge of his senses.

Nyx? He couldn't be sure. It felt like lightning.

Darius thought back to what the queen had said. Did Nyx have his powers? If so, how? He couldn't imagine how his power might have passed to her.

"We'll have to swim our way back to the ship." Jinx took to the air and shook off water. "Make sure no one follows us."

"There must be a way to get to Lyra." Azura gritted her teeth. "Maybe we can go back and—"

"We are not going back," Dahlia snapped. "I know how much you want your mother returned to you, but we can't risk going near those mind whisperers again."

Azura kept a hold of him as they swam. She shifted into her mer form and dragged him along beside her as they headed down the river. Her long tail slapped against him more than once. "How did your mind whisperer become so powerful?"

"They must be related to the queen." Dahlia paddled harder to keep up. Bones lagged behind them, and Jinx flew alongside Azura. "She must have either created them through magic or they are her children."

"You need to let me go. You tried to get her and failed. I'm no use to you now," Darius told Azura. "You wouldn't want to make an enemy of them, believe me. You know how powerful the queen is. Don't be foolish enough to think you can go against her daughters."

"If you can't help me rescue my mother, then you can at least help us get through the shield. Jinx has been watching them. They can't get out of the shield, either. If we can get free, we will never have to worry about the mind whisperers again." Azura glanced behind him. "Bones, keep up."

"Not all of us can swim as well as you, little sister." Bones huffed as he fought the churning current.

"Hurry, I want to get as far away from those girls as possible. Tell me, druid, how can I stop your lifemate?"

He coughed as water kept filling his nose and mouth. Darkness threatened to drag him under again. His bones ached from the iciness of the river. Even his blood ran cold.

"Not again." Azura slapped him. "Stay awake."

"I — I can't…" His head lolled to one side and his eyes closed. Light flashed around his body as his soul rose out of it. *This can't be good.*

Why did this keep happening? He couldn't be that close to death. Yet somehow his spirit kept leaving his body.

"Druid, wake up." Azura shook him.

Darius's spirit reappeared, standing on the bank. "That won't work." He held out his hands. Was it possible he hadn't died? Was this some newfound ability? He couldn't be sure.

Azura didn't respond to him. She couldn't see his spirit. This was the chance he needed to call for help.

"Nyx? Sirin?" he called out and whistled for his dragon.

The mermaid slapped him again. "Dahlia, you need to revive him again."

He winced at the harsh sound. "Would you stop doing that?" Darius reached out to touch his body, but couldn't re-emerge with it. Damn. "Sirin, come to me. Now!"

A shadow darkened the sky line and blotted out the sun as Sirin appeared over the treeline. The dragon sent a column of fire straight towards the mermaid.

Azura screamed and dragged his body under.

"Sirin, get my body out of the water!" Darius waved his arms at her. "I don't have any magic." Or at least he didn't think he had magic. He couldn't be sure Sirin could hear him, but he hoped she would. He'd used all his energy against the queen. Sirin shot out another burst of fire at the water. "Stop that! Holy spirits, I need Nyx."

Without magic, how could he reach her? He had used all of his strength against the queen.

Sirin dove into the water. A funnel of water rose and knocked the dragon against the side of the riverbank.

"Nyx, I need you." If he died, he'd never get the chance to say goodbye to her.

Green orbs swirled as Nyx appeared. Relief washed over him until he realised she had red lightning bolts etched across her face. They almost looked like blood.

Nyx raised her hand and sent lightning bolts hurtling towards Azura and her crew.

Darius didn't need to be near her to feel the fury and power burning around her. That couldn't be right. His Nyx never acted like this. He'd known her for almost two years and she'd never acted this way.

Azura and her crew all screamed as Nyx raised her hands and pulled all of them out of the water with her power. Even Dahlia struggled against Nyx's power.

"Nyx, stop!" Darius went towards her. Her eyes had turned black. The closer he got, the more her fury burned through him.

For a moment, her gaze flicked towards him before she turned and lightning shot from her hands.

The queen had been right. His druid powers had gone to her.

"Please don't do this!" Bones doubled over, his skin flashing with stone.

He wondered what was wrong with Nyx. Her eyes didn't look natural. He had seen her lose control of her powers before, but it had never been like this.

Sirin flew towards the back and landed. *Nyx?* The dragon sounded concerned.

"Sirin!" Darius called out for his dragon. "Hear me."

Sirin turned her head. *Darius?*

"Finally. What is wrong with Nyx?"

Her sisters called it the blood rage. They said if she doesn't come out of it, she will become like one of the damned.

Blood rage. A song rang through his mind from his childhood that the bards used to sing.

Beware beware, the one with eyes black as night. Beware beware innocents shall run in fright, for she will bear the lines of blood.

Havoc shall befall onto thee that none can stop. Doomed are thee who meets the touch of she.

Beware beware, her touch will destroy thee, beware beware your soul shall no longer belong to thee…

Darius knew there was more to the tale, but he couldn't remember the rest.

"Sirin, get my body." Darius willed himself to go back. A few moments later, he gasped, inhaling water. Sirin dove under and he grabbed onto her back. "Hurry…" he choked out. "Get me to Nyx."

What if she turns on you? She's not herself anymore.

"I'll bring her out of it… Somehow…" His teeth chattered as a cold wind blew over him. In truth, he didn't know how to bring her out of it.

Sirin shot over towards Nyx. When she landed, Darius leaned on his dragon for support as he slid off her back.

"Nyx, you need to stop." He stumbled as he moved away from Sirin and stood between Nyx and the crew. "I know you're angry, but don't do this. They are not bad people."

"Stay out of my way," she snarled and raised her hand again. Her power reverberated through the air like thunder without sound.

Darius flinched from the force and caught hold of her. "Nyx, your power doesn't work on me. It never has. Please come back to me." He touched her cheek. "You can stop whatever caused this."

Nyx shoved his hand away and pushed past him, intent on getting to Azura and her crew.

Druid, be careful. She is in — Niamh reached out to him with her mind.

I know. Tell me how to stop this!

Believe me, we have tried to talk to her. But she is not in her right mind anymore.

"Nyx." He grabbed her arm. Somehow, he had to get through to her.

She turned and more power reverberated through her. Lightning jolted between them.

Darius gasped as his power flowed back into him. "I love you." He couldn't think of anything else to say but the truth. He needed her to know how he felt.

Nyx winced as power jolted through her. She blinked, and the darkness vanished from her eyes. "You're alive." Nyx threw her arms around him and buried her face against his chest.

Darius wrapped his arms around her, glad to finally feel her back in his arms. He felt whole and complete again. And not just because he had his powers back.

He took a deep breath, breathing in the familiar scent of her. "I'm glad you heard me."

"Don't ever do that to me again." She gave him a shove. "I thought you were dead. And I — I can't be without you."

She hadn't said *I love you* back to him. But in that moment, he didn't care. All that mattered was he with her again.

He pulled her close again, glad for the warmth of her body. "I think your runes saved me."

"Don't give yourself up for me again, either." She pulled him in for a kiss.

He returned her kiss and deepened it.

"Let us go!" a voice yelled at them.

He and Nyx pulled away from each other to find Azura and her crew still under Nyx's power.

"I almost forgot about them." Nyx scowled and raised her hand.

Darius grabbed her wrist. "Don't. Let them go."

"They killed you!"

"No, they didn't. I'll explain more later. Just let them go."

Yes, they did. They almost drowned you, Sirin huffed. *I saw it. They took you away from me and Nyx!*

"They kept me alive after they captured me." Darius took her hand. "Let them go. They're trapped here just like us."

"But —"

"Please, Nyx. Killing them wouldn't do any good."

She gritted her teeth as she stomped over to the riverbank. "If you hurt my druid again, I will kill you," she snarled.

"I swear I won't hurt him." The mermaid whimpered.

"Good. You must be the mermaid Ambrose told us about." Nyx crossed her arms.

"I am Azura and this is my crew. You must be his lifemate."

Her eyes widened at the mermaid's words. "I am his…"

Arrows shot through the air. Darius spun around, surprised to finally have his senses working again.

"Argh, not again." Nyx groaned and released Azura and her crew from her hold on them.

Nyx waved her hand, so the arrows fell to the ground.

"Who is attacking us?" Darius raised his hand, glad when static shot through his fingers.

"Outsiders. Not everyone was forced out like we thought. A lot of the queen's prisoners were left behind."

"Oh. I've heard of them."

Several Outsiders charged from out of the trees.

"Stop!" a voice boomed around them. A man with long dark hair etched with grey stepped out. He raised a glowing wooden staff with a crystal on it that looked like Ambrose's. "You will not harm them."

"But they —" one of the Outsiders protested.

"I know who they are and they won't be a threat. Leave now." The man motioned for them to leave.

To Darius' surprise, the Outsiders ran off and disappeared into the trees.

The man strode over to them.

"Taliesin." Azura smiled. "Good, you're here. They —"

"Azura, you know better than to keep people in the water for so long. All of you know better." Taliesin glanced around the fallen crew.

"I didn't — I kept him alive."

The man came over to them. "You must be Nyx and Darius. I wondered when you would show up."

Nyx narrowed her eyes. "You know us? Who are you?"

"I am to Taliesin, a fellow druid. The first, in fact. And I know who you and Darius are, Nyx. Some of us have been waiting for you for a very long time." Taliesin motioned for them to follow him. "Come, we should get out of the open before the Nigax attacks."

"The what?"

"Shadow creatures. You two have put yourself in unnecessary danger by coming here."

"We didn't have a choice. And why should we trust you?" Nyx demanded.

163

"He's the first druid.;" He'd always thought Taliesin had been a myth. But they both knew immortals were real.

"That doesn't mean we can trust him," she hissed.

"Ambrose warned me you might come. I'm not a threat to either of you. Besides, I have no power. You should sense that for yourself."

Nyx furrowed her brow. "Just because I don't sense anything doesn't mean you don't have power. You have that." She motioned to the staff.

"I have a little power from this, but it powers in comparison to my true power." Taliesin held up his hand. "You can touch me and see for yourself."

Darius cast his senses out. It felt good to be back in full power. "He's telling the truth. But I don't sense any power from you. I have never met a druid without any power."

"I'm happy to answer all of your questions, but not out here in the open. Come." Taliesin motioned for them to follow him again.

CHAPTER 22

Taliesin transported them to a small house deep in the woods. Sirin hadn't been happy when Taliesin told her the woods were too dense for her. Nyx hadn't been happy either, but she didn't sense any threat from the other druid.

The dwelling barely had enough room for them to stand up in. Taliesin led them over to a small hearth.

"Would you like some tea?" The druid asked.

"We'd like some answers." Nyx sat down on a wooden bench beside Darius and took his hand. It felt good to be near him again. Like a missing part of her had been returned.

"As I said earlier, Ambrose told me you would come. I know who both of you are." Taliesin fumbled around and poured water into a pot, then set it over the fire. "He also said you would probably come here if anything happened to him. I didn't expect it to be so soon."

"How do you know Azura?" Darius let go of her hand and wrapped an arm around her, pulling her close. Nyx leaned in to him. She wouldn't let him go again.

"I have known her since the queen brought her here when she was a child. She is Lyra's daughter, and I helped to raise her. I felt like I had a responsibility to at least do that. Especially given all the damage Evony has done."

"Lyra has a daughter?" That didn't make sense, but she would ask about that another time.

I will tell you about her later, Darius told her in thought.
Good, we have a lot to talk about.

"What else did Ambrose tell you?" Darius asked Taliesin.

"Just to help you in any way I can when you came to me." Taliesin poured some water into a cup and mixed whatever was inside it. "I'm sure you already know the shield is failing. How do we fix it?" He picked up two more cups. "Are you sure you don't want some?"

"No thank you. Do you know how we can control the shield?" Nyx asked.

"Only the queen and Ambrose could do that."

"You must have been close to the queen. You must know something about it," Darius remarked. "My father used to tell me tales of how you were an adviser to the queen during her reign."

Taliesin laughed. "That feels like a lifetime ago."

"If Ambrose told you we would come to you for help, what else did he say? He left me a message, but he didn't explain very much." Nyx wouldn't mention the grimoire or what else Ambrose's message had said. She wouldn't be so quick to trust a stranger.

"He said the two of you might start becoming more powerful as the bond between you grew stronger." Taliesin sipped his tea. "I see that is true since you have a new ability, Darius."

Nyx's eyes widened. "What new ability?"

Darius rubbed the back of his neck. "I think so, yes. My spirit has left my body a few times whilst I was being held by the pirates."

"Pirates? Ha. Why would they even take you?"

He shrugged. "I landed in the river after I came through the shield on the day we were forced to flee from my castle.

Azura found me and saved me." He turned to the other druid. "Did you say we have a bond?"

Taliesin nodded. "Of course you do. You have been connected to each other for many years. I'm surprised you didn't realise it before now."

"But how could we be connected to each other? We only met when he came to Joriam to take me into custody." Living in Joriam and being falsely accused of Harland's murder felt like a lifetime ago now. "My powers haven't grown. At least I don't think they have."

Taliesin chuckled. "You went into the blood rage earlier today. I would say your powers have very much grown. Few mind whisperers ever had the ability to do that."

Blood rage. So that was what happened to her. She had heard her sisters talking about it, but at the time she had been so gripped in the fury of the rage she hadn't taken much of it in.

Nyx shook her head. "I know the blood rage is bad, but I don't know what it is. Niamh said it was something uncontrollable."

"A mind whisperer can only enter the blood rage when someone you love dies or they are threatened by danger. Tapping into the darker side of your gift makes your power almost limitless. Even someone with a shield would be susceptible to your control," Taliesin explained. "A century ago, when there were many mind whisperers, it was almost unheard of for one of them to enter such a state."

Someone you love. Darius had told her he loved her. That had brought her back to her senses. She had been too stunned to say anything, though. She didn't even know how to feel about his revelation.

"The two of you need to be careful now your abilities are growing. The bond between you makes you both much stronger. Having such power can be dangerous to yourselves and to other people."

"I don't understand why I would have a new ability. I should be too old for that. But I know my sorcery became much stronger when I was separated from my druid powers," Darius remarked.

"At least I gave you your powers back." Nyx breathed a sigh of relief. "Is he really going to become the next Archdruid? Lucien and the queen's guardian said they could sense that power in me when I had his abilities." She motioned to Darius.

Darius snorted. "I can't be the next Archdruid. I'm not his oldest son."

"We both know the power of the Archdruid passes down the Valeran bloodline. The oldest child doesn't always become the heir. Erthea chooses who is next in line. Besides, you are both part of the prophecy. If you came close to death recently, it could have triggered your new power. Especially since your father tried taking your powers from you." Taliesin motioned to the glowing runes on Darius' chest. "Nyx, do you know what these are?"

"Protection runes, I think." In truth, she didn't know what they were. Random runes often came to her, but that didn't mean she knew what they meant.

"Indeed, they are. They kept him alive by tying your life force to his in a deeper way than before."

Her mouth fell open. "What? I never meant for that to happen."

"Perhaps not. That's why you must be careful when using the ancient magics."

"I still can't become the next Archdruid. My father would never allow that. He uses his children as vessels and takes over their bodies." Darius grimaced.

Taliesin's eyes widened. "I'm surprised you know that. Few people do. Sooner or later, Fergus will be stopped. I have faith that destiny will take care of that. No Archdruid is meant to stay in power forever."

"Why are you trapped here?" Nyx asked.

"The queen bound my powers and imprisoned me. She said it was to protect me from the Archdruid. Only she can unbind me."

"How come you have that staff? That has some power." She motioned to it.

"Indeed, but it's limited. Ambrose broke part of his crystal off to allow me to have power again." Taliesin sat by a small fireplace. "At least enough to protect myself with."

"Are the Outsiders all prisoners or descendants of them?"

"Most are prisoners. Some of them are their descendants. They've grown over the last century.

"Are they bad?"

"They keep to themselves. Their leader, Cassian, won't be very welcoming. Those who live among them are taken care of. Those who choose to live separate are ostracised. Like me and Azura. You could try to befriend them, but they will view you as a threat."

Nyx, where are you? Niamh asked. *We can't sense you very well. Are you alright?*

I'm fine. I am with Darius and another druid.

Good, come home soon.

"Do you know how we can restore the shield and stop the queen?" Nyx asked.

"To do that, the two of you will need to work together. I will offer what help I can put this is a battle only you can win."

After leaving Taliesin, they headed back to the palace. Night had fallen. Once they'd had some food and talked with the others for a while, Nyx took him up to her chambers.

"Are you sure you're alright?" Nyx asked as she led Darius into the bath chamber. "Maybe you should rest awhile."

"The only thing I want is a good wash and get the grime of the river off me."

"I still don't know why you would let me vanquish your captors."

"They didn't hurt me and they're on our side." Darius pulled off his oversized shirt and tossed it to the floor.

"Did you miss the part about where they killed you and tried to rescue the queen?" Nyx sat down at the edge of the bath. The bath appeared more like a pool since it was big and deep enough to swim in.

Darius stripped off and dove under the water. Re-emerging a while later. "No one killed me. I cast a spell to stop my heart. The other times was me using my new ability."

"So your new ability is to make yourself die?"

He laughed and shook his head. She didn't find it funny. "No. Somehow my spirit can leave my body and travel some distance away from it. It will take some practice but it could become useful. I have seen my mother use the same ability."

"Those people still held you prisoner." Nyx scowled. "Why Ambrose thinks we should ally with them, I'll never understand."

"You spoke to Ambrose? When?" His eyes widened.

She shook her head. "He left me a message, along with the queen's grimoire." She rose, then hesitated. She didn't want to let him out of her sight for fear he might disappear again.

"Why don't you join me?" Darius grinned.

Nyx flushed red. "I can't."

"Why not? It's been a long few days. I might fall asleep and drown."

She scoffed. "You're not leaving me again. Not even in death. If you do, I will come and drag you back."

"Is that a promise, love?"

Love. He never called her that.

"Yes. I – I can't be without you."

"Why not?" Darius reached up and stroked her hair off her face, sending water dripping down her cheek. "You're all I could think about whilst I was gone."

Nyx gripped his hand and sighed. "You know why."

"No, I don't. I need to hear you say it."

"You're important to me. I hope that mermaid realises you're my druid."

Darius chuckled. "She does. I already told her that." He pulled her in for a kiss. "I meant what I said to you earlier. I do love you. You don't have to say it back. I just needed to tell you."

Nyx hesitated and pulled away. "I need to tell you something."

"I'm listening."

"The shield is failing. If we don't find a way to keep your father out, my sisters and I —" She swallowed, her throat dry. "We can't stay here. We'll have to run."

"I know that."

"Which means we… We might not be able to see each other anymore."

Darius scoffed. "You're not leaving without me."

"Andovia is your home."

"I don't need a home. I need you." He captured her mouth in a kiss.

Nyx wrapped her arms around him. Images flashed through her mind. The link was still there. It hadn't broken.

After a few moments, she pulled away.

Darius groaned. "I hate it when you do that."

"You're getting me all wet." She rose and tugged her tunic, tossing aside, then pulled off her hose and slid out into the water. Its warmth wrapped around her like a welcoming embrace.

Darius slipped his arms around her from behind, trailing his lips down her neck. "I missed you… So much."

She smiled. "I missed you too." She ran her fingers over the runes she had put on his chest.

"Why didn't you tell me about them?"

"I didn't have time to before your mother came. We should come up with new rules."

"What kind of rules?"

"Like… How you're not to sacrifice yourself for me again?"

"I can't promise that. I'd die for —"

"Don't say that." Her body went rigid. "I won't leave you. I can't. We are either in this together or not."

"We are, love."

Nyx woke up a few hours later. Her dreams are haunted by more memories of being buried. She slipped out of Darius's embrace.

She pulled out the queen's grimoire and flicked through it. There had to be something in there about the shield.

She sat on the seat in the queen's chamber. A green orb hovered over her.

How did the queen power the shield?

"Nyx?" Darius appeared in the doorway.

Smoke billowed, and the Guardian appeared.

"Gemmill, don't you dare touch my druid!" Nyx shot to her feet. "He's my lifemate." She wedged herself between Darius and the Guardian.

Gemmill's mouth opened and closed. "But he's the —"

"The son of the Archdruid. Yes, how shocking." She rolled her eyes.

"He is your enemy."

"No, I'm not." Darius wrapped a protective arm around her waist. *Who is he?*

The queen's guardian. Don't tell him where she is. Nyx took Darius' hand. *Let's go.*

"Why does he call you Nyx?" Gemmill frowned at her. "Only your sisters call you by that name."

"Because he does." She held out her free hand for the book. It flew into her grasp.

Gemmill winced. "The shield is faltering. It's already diminished. Parts of the city have fallen."

"How do you know that?" Nyx furrowed her brow.

"I sense it. How can you not know that?"

"I knew it was failing, but I don't know how to stop it." Nyx tucked the book under her arm.

"Then how can you let him in here?" Gemmill glared at Darius.

"I'm not my father. We're bonded."

Gemmill gave a harsh laugh. "The queen would never allow that."

"The queen doesn't rule me. There must be some way to control it." Nyx gripped the book tighter.

"Ask your mother. You must know where she is. You and your sisters don't seem to be doing anything to find her."

"We're too busy trying to stop her from killing us," Nyx snapped.

"She's in that well, isn't she?" Gemmill's dark eyes narrowed.

"How do we control the shield?"

"Only your mother can do that."

"My mother let me and my sisters die. She never came for us when we came back, either. She can rot for all I care."

"I won't let my queen suffer." Gemmill lunged for them.

Darius raised his hand and Gemmill hit a wall of energy.

How did you do you do that? Nyx arched an eyebrow. *I can't use my magic on him.*

He shrugged. *Taliesin was right when he said our powers were growing.*

"You will not contact the queen or go near here, understood?" Nyx glared at the guardian.

Gemmill vanished in a whirl of smoke.

Nyx led him out of the room. Now "how did you do that? My powers don't work on him. Neither did your powers when I tried them."

"I'm stronger when I'm with you. Plus, I've been using my sorcery more."

"But you hate that."

"I do, but it's part of me. Just as much as being a druid is."

"Aren't you worried about losing control?"

"My link to you kept me grounded. You don't mind we have a bond?"

She shook her head. "No." She touched his cheek. "One day, we'll seal our bond."

He grinned and squeezed her hand. "Yes, we will."

"I found out my name was Aerin. Strange. It doesn't feel like my name."

"Have you remembered anything else?"

"Just the queen's secret word for Gemmill. I need to remember more. I can only do that in death. Will you help me?"

"To die? No. Absolutely not."

"Not for long. Just so I can remember more."

"Nyx, dying isn't healthy. What if you can't come back?"

"If you cast a spell on me, you can send me into death."

Darius didn't look convinced. "I'm pulling you back if something goes wrong."

"I'll be fine. Just do it."

"Maybe it would be safer to do this with your sisters."

She shook her head. "No, I don't want to risk them. Just do it."

He hesitated. "I don't like this."

"It's the only way I have of remembering my life before I came, became Nyx. Please, just do it."

He sighed. "You better come back to me."

"I will. You'll be stuck with me forever." She flashed him a smile.

Darius chanted the spell and Nyx slumped against him as the spell dragged her under.

Nyx found herself sitting in a bright room. A book lay open in front of her. Her sisters sat at tables nearby. Niamh chewed on the end of her hair and Novia tapped her foot.

"Girls, have you read through the passage yet?" Taliesin strolled over to them.

What was he doing here? Had she known him?

She needed to know about the shield. Not remember some random lesson. But she couldn't control what came back to her.

The memory changed. She found herself back in the temple the day the city had been taken.

The temple doors burst open as the Archdruid and his guards marched in.

One of the guards grabbed her arm. She screamed and let her power reverberate through the air.

The guard flinched. "My Lord, what do you want us to do with the queen's children?"

"Lock them up until I'm done with the queen."

Nyx screamed, forcing her power to rise again.

The guard doubled over, clutching his ears. Light flashed around her as she transported out.

She reappeared in the woods.

Nyx gasped as her body dragged her out of the memory. "No, send me back."

"I can't. You need time to recover."

"But I remembered the day of the siege. Your father stormed into the temple, but I got out. I went into the forest. I need to see what happens next."

"You know you can't stay dead for too long or your death will be permanent."

"One other thing I saw, Taliesin knew me as Aerin."

CHAPTER 23

"I think we should all sit and talk with Azura and her crew," Darius said as they sat around the dining hall the next morning eating breakfast. "We need allies if we stay here. And you said you're Azura's friend. Maybe you can talk to her."

Niamh leaned back in her chair and sipped her rakka tea. "She was my friend a long time ago. But she almost got us all killed when her crew went for the queen."

"Lyra is Azura's mother. That's the only reason she came for her."

Niamh's mouth fell open. "How is that possible? She was a child when I knew her. Around twelve. We trained together in the Order."

Niamh was still stunned to see is Azura here of all places.

"So Azura is an assassin like you?" Nyx frowned.

Darius shook his head. "I don't think she's a killer. She didn't harm me."

"I beg to differ," Nyx scoffed. "She still kept you a prisoner. Somehow, I don't think we should trust what Ambrose says either."

"Azura trained to be a spy, not an assassin," Niamh remarked. "She doesn't have what it takes to do that. Azura made a good spy, from what I've heard."

"I don't think we should trust her or her crew." Novia grimaced. "They kidnapped me."

"They wouldn't have had much choice," Darius remarked. "The queen used them to do her bidding."

"How did Azura end up with the queen?" Nyx's frown deepened.

"From what I remember, someone bought her from the Order." Niamh bit her lip. "I was really sad when she went away. No one would tell me where she had gone."

"Even if we ally with this mermaid and her crew, then what?" Novia demanded.

"Maybe they can help us move the queen," Darius mused. "Their ship can travel underwater. It will allow us to get out of the city undetected."

"I'll talk to Azura —" Niamh froze as her senses prickled.

Nyx waved her hand, and a hologram of the city appeared. "The shield's retreated further."

"That's right where the Outsiders live," Niamh remarked.

"We better go and help them before the Dragon Guard kills them all." Darius rose to his feet.

"But they said they didn't want our help," Niamh pointed out.

"Just because they don't want our help doesn't mean they won't get it."

"Guess we're going then." Niamh conjured her pack and grabbed more knives from it.

"Lucien and Ranelle can stay and keep watch on the queen," Nyx added. "We can't risk her getting out."

"I'm coming too," Novia added.

Niamh frowned at her. "You're supposed to be confined to the palace."

"You need me to help the other dragons. They trust me."

We need all the people we can get, Nyx said.

Fine, but we need to watch her.

Novia scowled. *I heard that.*

Niamh readied herself for a fight as she, her sisters, and Darius appeared near the Outsiders' camp. Chaos played out below them. People and dragons guards were everywhere.

Protect the Outsiders and force the guards back through the shield, Nyx said and tossed Ambrose's staff to Darius. *See if you can use this. Try to force the shield to repel them, if you can.*

We are protecting the Outsiders? Baron sounded confused.

Niamh nodded. *So it seems. Come on, let's go.*

Dragon Guards ran on the ground and swarmed through the air.

Baron roared and sent a plume of fire straight at the first guard.

"I didn't know you could breathe fire," Niamh gasped.

I can now. I have my full strength back. Baron swooped lower and grabbed hold of a guard between his talons. The man screamed and thrashed as they headed straight for the shield and tossed the guard through it.

The guard's dragon roared and lunged for her and Baron.

Baron swerved. Niamh's mind linked with his — almost like they were one. She felt and saw what he did.

Baron, talk to the dragon. Try to tell him we won't hurt him if he joins us.

I can't reach his mind. There's a shield blocking it.

Damn the Archdruid!

They swerved out of the dragon's way, but the beast continued after them.

Why couldn't it leave them alone? They got rid of its rider. Niamh didn't like the idea of killing dragons, either. Knowing they could be potential allies.

She ordered Baron to follow her lead. As one, Baron swung and threw himself at the other dragon. Niamh released her power at the same time. They slammed into the other beast and thunder shook the air.

Baron, can you become bigger? Grab him!

Baron's body shifted beneath her as he grew and latched onto the other dragon.

The other beast thrashed and screamed.

Baron threw the other dragon towards the river where it crashed into the water.

Around her, Nyx, Darius, Novia and their dragons fought against the guards and attacking dragons.

Another dragon and its rider lunged for Azura as she hurled blasts of water at her assailants.

"Coming through!" Niamh and Baron thrashed against the Dragon Guard.

A while later, all the Dragon Guards were gone.

Niamh and Baron landed by Azura. "Are you alright?"

"You saved me."

"Of course I did. You're my friend." She couldn't deny part of her was happy to see Azura again.

Azura had been like a sister to her when they were kids.

"Am I? You're not angry at me over the druid?"

Niamh shrugged. "I'm not the one you need to prove yourself to. But you can't come after the queen again. If you do, we will stop you."

Azura shook her head. "I don't want the queen to go free. I just want my mother back."

Nyx and Novia landed in the camp.

"Thank you for helping us." Taliesin gave them a grateful nod.

"Helping? They're the ones who brought the Dragon Guard here," Cassian snapped.

"You're welcome." Niamh scowled. "We could just have let them kill you."

"Niamh," Novia hissed.

"If anyone needs healing or a place to stay, you're welcome to join us at the palace," Nyx told them. "The shield will keep receding and the Dragon Guard will come back."

"Listen to Ambrose's daughters, Cassian," Taliesin said. "It's better to be allies and enemies."

"We will never be allies with them." Cassian glared at the druid, then motioned his people away.

Niamh headed back to the palace with her sisters. "Are you sure it's wise to invite them here?" she asked.

Nyx shook her head. "We can't leave them to the mercy of the Archdruid."

"We can't have a load of people around that the queen might be able to use against us, either." Niamh crossed her arms. "She's already gotten to Novia once already. What is to stop her from getting to someone else? We don't have time to watch over dozens of people. It's safer if they stay away from us."

"She has a point," Novia agreed. "We can't put innocent lives at risk."

To Niamh's surprise, Azura came in. "You said you wanted to talk." She gave Niamh a nervous look. "I also came to offer my services."

"Your services? For what?" Nyx sneered. "Kidnapping people?"

Nyx. Niamh shot her a glare.

Azura winced. "I'm sorry… For that and for almost releasing the queen. I am a healer. If anyone needs help, I'm at your disposal."

"You're welcome to help out," Darius added.

"Niamh said you need help to move the queen. My crew —"

Nyx scoffed. "You really expect us to trust you? How do we know you won't just make off with her?"

Azura's lip curled. "The queen can burn for all I care. I wish the Archdruid had killed her. I just want my mother back."

Ada came into the hall carrying healing supplies.

"Ada, why don't you make us some tea?" Darius suggested as the brownie walked by. "We can sit and talk. Azura, this is my… lifemate Nyx, and you have already met Niamh and Novia."

Novia glared at the mermaid. "Do you make a habit of kidnapping people?"

"I didn't have a choice. If I don't do, the queen tells me, she makes my mother suffer for it."

"How can Lyra be your mother?" Nyx furrowed her brow. "Are you a mind whisperer like us?"

All of them gathered around the table as Ada brought some tea in a few moments later.

Niamh flinched. She had always cared about Azura, but she didn't know how to feel about the possibility of having another sister. Was that possible?

Azura shook her head. "I'm half fae and half mermaid. It's… a long story of how my parents met. I only know small parts of it."

Niamh breathed a sigh of relief. "How old are you? I think you were around the age of twelve when you joined the Order."

"Twenty. I grew up in Althea until I was twelve. Then I spent time with the Order of Blood. They trained me… Until the queen 0rought me," Azura explained.

"But how? The queen has possessed Lyra for over a century. She —" Nyx asked.

"For a brief time, she left my mother. I don't know where she went. My mother stayed in Althea for a while and met my father. Not long after that I was born, then the queen took her again."

"Where's Althea?" Niamh frowned, unable to place the name.

"That's supposed to be a myth," Darius answered.

"It's not. It's one of several cities in the undersea," Azura explained. "The queen went there a few times. She said she was looking for someone. One of the Twelve — whoever they are."

"The Twelve were a group of immortals. Some say the first magickind," Darius replied.

"Were? Azura frowned.

"The Archdruid overthrew them. We think he keeps them somewhere and harnesses their power," Nyx remarked.

Niamh glanced around at the other crew members. "What about the rest of your crew? How did you come to be here? You weren't in the Order of Blood."

"I was a pirate. The queen's forces captured my ship," Bones explained. "I have been her prisoner for the last century."

"I'm from Andovia. Born and raised in Varden Forest." Jinx settled on the table. "The queen picked sprites to be her spies, since we can blend in so well. It was an honour to be chosen." Jinx scowled. "I just didn't think I'd been enslaved for an entire century."

"I'm Dahlia. I've been here as long as I can remember. Ilari are treated as worse than slaves and demons." Dahlia scowled. "Most rulers seek to lock us up or use us."

"I don't sense the queen's power over all of you. If she used her touch on you, you can lose your will," Nyx said.

"The queen can't take our souls with her power. But her touch works on Bones and Jinx to an extent." Azura grimaced. "Dahlia and I are immune from her touch. She uses people we love to get us to do her bidding. Believe us when we tell you we want her gone more than anything."

"Stopping her is a lot more difficult than you'd imagine." Niamh leaned back in her chair.

"Can you get the queen spirit out of Lyra's body?" Azura glanced around the table, hopeful.

"We will damn well try."

CHAPTER 24

A few days passed, Darius enjoyed getting to know Azura and her crew better. Nyx still acted hesitant around them, but she'd come around. Azura and the others had been helpful in telling them about the queen.

He awoke to find Nyx gone from their bed again.

One thing they hadn't managed so far was to unlock the queen's vault. The door refused to open. That hadn't surprised him. His father was paranoid about anyone getting into his vault.

He climbed out of bed and headed into the other chamber, where he found Nyx with the grimoire. "Shouldn't you get some sleep?"

"No, not when we have the queen and a failing shield to worry about. There has to be a way to stop an immortal."

"Ambrose would know. Perhaps Taliesin can help. We'll see him again in the morning."

"Azura wants to know if we can save Lyra, too."

"I think she knows Lyra might be lost."

"How did your father subdue the Twelve? If we knew how to do that..." Nyx lowered the grimoire.

"I wish I knew. I doubt my father would share that secret with anyone."

"Maybe your gran would know. She knew about Fergus."

"Her mind is too fragmented. I still keep thinking about

185

Ambrose. Wondering if I really knew him." Darius didn't want to bother his grandmother again. It had been hard enough to get the answers out of her the last time they had gone to visit her.

"Maybe we can contact him."

"How? My father has him."

"His mind still exists — despite what the queen did to him. Let's try a spell."

"I'm not sure a spell is strong enough to get through my father and the queen's magic." Darius shook his head. "Let's try." He sat down beside her.

"It's too bad we can't go and visit your father's vault," Nyx remarked.

They went back to their bed and chanted the spell together.

A few moments later, they appeared outside in the forest. Not what Darius had expected. Trees arched over them and a thick, heavy canopy blackened out most of the sunlight. Small cracks of light crept through.

"This isn't far from the forest where Azura and her crew are docked." He took Nyx's hand.

"We are supposed to connect to Ambrose. Why are we here?" Nyx furrowed her brow.

"You two shouldn't be here." Ambrose appeared behind them. "How did you even reach me?"

The spell must be working, Darius said.

Yes, but how do we know it's him? It could be your father or some part of the queen's magic.

The queen is locked up. If she can reach Novia, she can reach Ambrose as well.

I don't sense my father's magic.

"We need your help," Darius explained. "We need to know how to strengthen the shield."

"Only the queen can control that. You must have got my message."

"We know I'm your daughter." Nyx glowered at their former mentor. "There must be a way to make the shield stronger."

"There isn't. Nyx, I'm —" Ambrose reached out for her.

Nyx took a step back. "Save your worthless apologies. We didn't come here for that. Just give us some answers."

"Where is the queen's body?" Darius persisted. "We need to move her from the well. When my father comes, he'll go straight for her."

Ambrose shook his head. "Evony is immortal. You can't contain her unless it's in a void where she would be rendered powerless. Or an impenetrable prison. But such a thing is impossible."

"The Archdruid imprisoned the other Twelve. Think, Ambrose, what did he do to them?"

Ambrose paced. "Evony said something about a crystal — a weapon that overpowered her kind. She was a child when it happened. The only one who would truly know is her parents."

Can you hear his thoughts? Darius asked. *Or get anything from his mind? I'm not sure we can trust him anymore.*

I haven't trusted him in months. I'm trying to get something from him, but his thoughts are jumbled.

"She has parents?" Nyx gaped at him.

"Of course she does. You don't expect immortals to have sprung up out of the ground, do you?" Ambrose gave a harsh laugh. "Taliesin and the Great Guardian are her parents."

Darius' mouth fell open. "Taliesin was her prisoner."

"Indeed. She viewed him as a threat, so she rendered him powerless. He would be the one to ask. No one knows more about the immortals than him."

187

"What about the queen's body? Where is it?" Nyx repeated.

"I will never reveal that to anyone. If you want to stop Evony, the best thing to do is to restore her to her body so she can reactivate the shield. Then render her powerless, but that's almost impossible," Ambrose said. "You need to get me out of the Archdruid's custody. I'm the only one who can restore her."

Darius laughed. "That's impossible. No one escapes from the Archdruid."

"If anyone could do it, it's the two of you. You are part of the prophecy."

"Then why were you so adamant about us not being together?" Nyx demanded.

"Because I feared how powerful you both would become when you're together. You have been connected to each other from the beginning." Ambrose sat down on a log. "Get me out of here. Taliesin could help you break the queen's hold on me."

"How do we get into the queen's vault?" Nyx persisted.

"Use the combination I left you in my message."

"Your message ended before we had a chance to get it. So what is the right combination?" Nyx crossed her arms.

"I…I don't remember. Evony must have known I would leave things to help you with. Damn her. See if Taliesin can help you."

Darius and Nyx headed down the next morning to summon Taliesin.

Nyx waved her hand and the other druid appeared in a flash of light. "You could call first."

"She does that all the time." Niamh and Novia sat down with them.

"What did you summon me?" Taliesin furrowed his

brow.

"Are you really the queen's father?" Nyx asked.

He gaped at them. "You remember that."

"Ambrose told us." Nyx shook her head. "Why didn't you mention that?"

"Because I couldn't. Ambrose only told me to tell you what you needed to know."

"Why? Do you know why we can't remember our past?" Niamh demanded.

"I'm not the one you should ask. The Great Guardian is."

"Is she the one who erased our memories?" Nyx's eyebrows rose.

"I can't answer that. Why did you summon me?" He repeated.

"Ambrose said we need to restore Evony to restore her to her body."

"How can we move her somewhere more secure without her killing us?" Novia added.

"Why not use a collar? It's an ancient device marked with runes that can repress someone's power. It should be strong enough to render her powerless."

"Those are very hard to find," Darius remarked.

"Evony probably has some in her vault."

"We can't access that."

"Come with me." Taliesin motioned for them to follow him.

They headed up to the third floor.

Taliesin tapped the crystals, and the door swung open. "Be careful what you touch in here."

Darius and the sisters headed inside. The walls glittered with ivory and gold. Shelves lined them with books, scrolls and crystals. It reminded him of his father's vault.

"Hopefully we can find something in here that can help

with the shield," Nyx remarked.

Darius picked up some metal bracelets that he recognised as glamour devices. "That and a lot more."

CHAPTER 25

Nyx's head spun as she and her sisters scouted around the palace and its vast grounds. She wanted to see if they could find where they'd been buried. As if it would somehow give them more answers. Taliesin hadn't been able to tell them anything useful.

Niamh had gone to search the palace itself and Novia had gone to search the south side where she had moved the dragons to.

She stopped when she spotted the flames hovering over the well where the queen remained trapped. Like it or not, the queen had answers. Nyx crouched by the edge of the well. The queen wouldn't give up answers easily.

She closed her eyes and projected herself down there.

The queen lay slumped on the ground.

"Why don't my sisters and I remember who we are?" Nyx asked.

Lyra's eyes flew open. Her face had turned grey. "Water... Give me some. If you're going to leave me down here, you could at least nourish me. Look how weak this body is."

"That body can't die unless you leave it."

The queen's eyes closed and light shot out of Lyra's body. The queen, in her true fae form, appeared. "That's better. Why are you here?"

"Because you have answers I need. And you didn't

answer my question."

The queen paced back and forth. "I don't know why you and your sisters don't remember anything about your past. Nor do I know how or why you came back."

"You didn't bring us back?" Nyx frowned.

The queen snorted. "Of course not. If I could revive the dead, I would be back in my own body by now." She continued to pace around the small space. "Look at that pathetic husk." She motioned towards Lyra's body, then reached for Nyx.

Nyx stepped back as lightning flashed between them.

The queen flinched. "I sense Valeran power connected to you. Have you bound yourself to that druid?"

She smirked. "So what if I have? I trust him more than I'll ever trust you."

"You're a fool then. Love will bring you nothing but pain. I was foolish enough to fall for your father's lies. Don't think the Valeran won't to do the same to you," Evony spat. "I thought I raised you better than that."

"You didn't raise me. A murdering, abusive thief did. If you are as powerful as everyone claims, why didn't you stop the Archdruid? Why didn't you force him out instead of jumping into Lyra's body?" she demanded. "You're immortal. I thought you were invincible."

Evony scoffed. "Immortal, yes, but I am one person. The Archdruid has the strength of the other Twelve on his side. Against that I am nothing."

"You must know something about how or why we came back. Did Ambrose do something?"

Evony laughed. "Ambrose has been under my control since the day you were murdered. I made sure of that. The bastard thought he could betray me and get away with it."

"That doesn't mean you have full control over him. He didn't always act like a man who was enslaved." She had seen that in what little fragmented memories she had recovered.

Evony laughed harder. "You poor little girl. You have no idea what our power is capable of. Nor do you have the strength to use it to its full potential. If you had any sense, you'd find a way to take control of the Valeran. Instead, you're too busy fawning over each other."

Nyx gritted her teeth. Damn, there had to be a way to get answers out of her. She had used her power against spirits before. Maybe she could use it along with Darius' magic.

"Verum dico." She had never used spirit magic before since that was sorcery and didn't come from nature. But if her bond to Darius was as strong as everyone thought, she should be able to access his powers. Legend said that was another part of being bonded to someone.

Evony flinched. "What are you doing?"

"You use your power to get what you want. Don't be surprised if I do the same." She crossed her arms. "So tell me, Mother, how can we get our memories back?"

"Like I said, I don't know how or why you came back. You and your sisters were dead after the Archdruid besieged my realm. I managed to force him out, but even I can't revive the dead." Something flickered in Lyra's eyes, but Nyx couldn't name the emotion. "Have you bound the Valeran to you?" Evony arched a brow.

"Of course not. My power doesn't work on him. I wouldn't use it even if it did."

"You must have done something or his power couldn't have transferred to you. Are you lovers?"

Her cheeks flushed. "No. You must know some way of getting our memories back. I searched your grimoire and I couldn't find anything in there that might help us."

"I will say it again. I don't know how or why you came

back. Let alone why you don't remember who you are. Perhaps it is a side-effect of coming back from the dead." Evony sneered. "I, for one, would like to know how you did that. Give me your hand."

"What?"

"If I can sense you, I might be able to help you find a solution."

Nyx hesitated. She knew she shouldn't let Evony anywhere near her. Even in spirit form. But she'd be careful and if Evony tried anything, she'd stop her.

"Zondus." She waved her hand and bound Evony's spirit in place.

Evony's eyes darkened. "What are you doing?"

"Making sure you don't try anything." Nyx took hold of her hand. "What do you sense?" It felt like touching something solid, but she didn't know how that was possible.

Evony gripped her fingers and energy jolted between them.

"Well?"

"Your — your link is stronger to him than I thought. That's how you came back." Evony gripped her hand tighter, and the light flashed between them.

Gods, Evony had started draining her. Nyx pulled her hand back, but Evony gripped her tighter. She gasped as she opened her eyes and her spirit reconnected with her body.

The flames over the well exploded as light blasted through them.

Oh no.

The light shot towards her as Evony's spirit reformed. "That's better."

Her mouth fell open. "You can't be out here."

Evony cackled. "If I'd known how easy it would be to

get you to do that, I would have done it weeks ago. You'll make a good new host." She gripped the sides of Nyx's head.

Nyx screamed as pain tore through her.

An image of Darius — a much younger Darius — stood and held out his hand as he pulled her out of the earth.

Nyx blasted the queen away from her.

Evony stumbled and grabbed her wrist. She yelped and backed away. "I should have known the Valeran's bond with you would protect you." Light sparkled around her as she transformed into a blur of golden orbs and shot into the air.

Darius appeared and ran over to her. "What's wrong? What happened?"

"She's out. Come on, we have to find her." She grabbed his hand and transported them out in a swirl of orbs.

CHAPTER 26

Darius' head spun as he and Nyx shot over the forest. The queen's golden orbs raced ahead of them and vanished int at the canopy of trees. They descended after her and reappeared near a row of wooden houses.

"Where are we?" He hadn't seen this part of the city in the past few days since he'd come through the shield. "And how did the queen get out?"

"Because… I was stupid. I never should have —" She blew out a breath. "I never should have gone to her for help."

"Why would you do that?"

"I asked her about me and my sisters. About why we don't remember our lives as her daughters."

Three men surrounded them. The ones she'd encountered before.

"How did you two get here?" The elf asked.

Darius gripped Nyx's hand. "We're looking for someone. Listen, we're not here to cause any trouble."

"That's too bad. Because you're trcspassing." The elf raised his bow.

I'll use my power on them, Nyx said.

No. What if one of them is possessed by your mother? It won't work.

She's not my mother. Nyx scowled. *Don't call her that. Shouldn't we use our powers to get them to back off?*

What do people fear more than the queen? Just stay close. Darius drew magic and his eyes blazed with power. No one could ignore the power of the Archdruid.

All three men backed away. "That ain't possible," said the troll. "The Archdruid hasn't come here in —"

"In the last century, since he took control of Andovia." Darius gave them a hard look. "The Archdruid is my father. Now I want to speak to your leader. Take us to him."

What are you doing? Why would you tell them who you are? Nyx furrowed her brow.

With the queen loose, we'll need all the help we can get. Don't you think they deserve to know who they're up against?

Yes, but we shouldn't tell them who you are.

Why? The shield is still up. It's not like they can go to my father.

Nyx scoffed. *Don't be so sure of that. The shield won't stay up forever. Not if your father has anything to do with it. Or the queen, for that matter.*

"Their leader is right here. I'm Cassian." A tall man with curly brown hair stepped out with several other people. "Oh, it's you two again. Why do you keep attacking my people?"

"Us? You attacked us more than once." Nyx crossed her arms.

The man turned his attention to her. "You and your sisters have attacked my people more than once. We've only protected ourselves."

"We came to warn you, the queen's back."

The Outsiders glanced at each other and some paled.

"The queen ain't coming back. She died —"

"Her body might have burnt, but her spirit didn't leave. She can possess anyone, and she will kill anyone who gets in her way," Nyx explained. "That's why all of you need to be careful."

"The queen can't come back," Cassian insisted. "That's just a legend to the Andovians made up to give them false hope."

"She's back and you're in danger," Darius said. "Not only from her, but from my father — the Archdruid."

"What do you expect us to do, then?" Cassian demanded.

"Ally with us. We can help each other out."

Cassian laughed. "You want me to send my people against the Archdruid? You're bloody mad!"

The other Outsiders laughed too.

"If we join forces, we could help protect you from the queen. Give you spells — protection so you can't be possessed by her."

"Possessed? You expect us —" Cassian scoffed.

"Believe what you like. Don't say we didn't warn you." Nyx tugged at his arm. *Druid, let's go. They won't help us.*

He sighed. *Wait, let's scan them first. See if we can sense the queen.*

If she's inside a body, I doubt we'll be able to.

They both cast their senses out.

No trace of the queen remained.

Maybe I should use my power to compel them into submission, Nyx mused. *If anyone is immune, we would know it could be her.*

How would we know? She would have access to the person's memories. Someone could be immune — not everyone is susceptible to your power.

Light exploded overhead and thunder boomed.

"When my father comes through, none of you will stand a chance against him. If you do need help, you can find sanctuary at the palace," Darius said.

He and Nyx transported out.

They reappeared a short distance away.

"I doubt they will ally with us," Nyx remarked.

"I don't think they're bad. We have a common enemy; we should work together."

"Let's focus on finding the shield room — Taliesin said something about the shield being controlled by a crystal. It has to be around here somewhere. And this is one area we haven't searched yet. My sisters are checking in the palace itself. It's a shame Ambrose isn't here."

"Did you learn anything from your — the queen?"

Nyx scowled. "Not much. I still can't believe I was stupid enough to let her trick me. She said she didn't know how or why we came back." Nyx hesitated. "I saw something when she touched me. A memory, I think." She pulled her hand away from his. "I remember you... Pulling me out of my tomb, I think you brought me back."

His mouth fell open. "What? How? I think I'd remember something like that."

She shrugged. "I don't know. I don't remember much either. The queen seemed just as stunned."

"Show me." Darius held out his hand.

She grasped his fingers, and both closed their eyes.

An image of Nyx coming through the earth and him pulling her out came to him.

"That's — why don't I remember that?" He frowned. "Someone must have erased my memory too."

"You have to be around twelve and I had to be ten — the same age as when I died." She grimaced.

"How? I can't bring anyone back from the dead. Even my father can't do that."

Bringing the dead back to life went against nature itself. Such magic was beyond dark. Most magickind forbade such practices. It wouldn't work anyway. Even magic had its limits.

"You must have done it somehow. We'll figure it out

later." Nyx then chanted a tracking spell.

His eyes widened. "You're getting good at casting spells."

"I learnt from the best." She flashed him a smile and yelped as she slammed into something invisible.

"What is that?" Darius reached out and found something hard. "It feels like a door."

"I don't know. Why is there a door in the middle of the forest?"

"Let's find out." Darius raised his hand, but nothing happened.

"Open." Nyx waved her hand and a glowing door appeared. "Let's go."

The door creaked open and appeared to be on the side of a hill.

"How did you do that?" Darius furrowed his brow.

"I — I think I know this place… Somehow." She led the way through the chamber and conjured an orb to light their way.

"It feels familiar to me too, but I don't remember being here."

Nyx frowned at the corner and froze. A large crypt stood on one side of the wall. An inscription hung above it. The crypt stood open and dirt had spilled out.

"Here lies Aerin, Ava and Anisa." She gasped as she read the inscription. "Gods, we have different names."

"Maybe whoever erased your memories gave you a new name. Someone had to have sent you out of Andovia."

"But why did they make us forget?"

He shook his head. "I don't know."

Nyx went over and peered into the empty crypt. "This is it. The place I keep seeing in my dreams. I was buried here for almost a century."

"But you came back. You have a second chance."

She blinked back tears. "I feel like I don't know who I am now."

"You're Nyx. You're the same person you've always been." He wrapped his arms around her and kissed her forehead. "That won't change."

"What if I turn out like her?"

"You're nothing like her."

"You don't know that. Ambrose loved her and looked at how that turned out." She pulled away from him and wiped away her tears. She ran a hand over the inscription. "Ambrose must've buried us here. He'd know where the shield room is and how to control it."

"Too bad we can't get him."

"Maybe we can."

CHAPTER 27

"You want us to go back to Alaris and rescue Ambrose?" Niamh's mouth fell open.

Nyx leaned back in her chair as they sat around the hall. "Yes, Ambrose is the only one who knows how to control the shield. And he could help us track the queen since he is still bound to her."

"Did you lose your mind when you found our tomb?" Niamh scoffed.

"No, *Ava*. And do you have a better idea?" Nyx put her hands on her hips.

"Don't call me that. That doesn't sound like my name." Niamh scowled. "I'm not changing my name. Plus, why would we save him?"

"Because he's our father. We can't let the Archdruid destroy him."

"But he helped the queen kidnap me from Glenfel." Novia crossed her arms. "I'm not sure I want to save him. He's not a good man. He's a killer."

"Little sister makes a good point," Niamh agreed. "I don't see why we should save him."

Nyx crossed her arms. "He's the only one who knows the queen and could help us stop her. He's not all bad. You don't know him like I do."

"He's under her control. What's to stop him from killing us?" Niamh gripped the edge of the table. "Let him rot with the Archdruid."

"We know he tried to save us before the Archdruid took the city. He loved us, and love can be stronger than our touch. If you don't want to come, Darius and I will go."

"Speaking of the druid, are we bound to him too?" Niamh arched an eyebrow.

"Of course not."

"He saved you, which in turn must've saved us," Novia pointed out.

She sighed. "Darius' magic didn't go to you. Just to me."

"Because you have a bond," Niamh said. "I, for one, don't ever want to be bound to anyone. Imagine being stuck with one man forever."

Novia grinned. "I think it's romantic."

Niamh snorted. "You've never been with a man. When you have, you'll realise you don't want to be stuck with one. Love doesn't last anyway. Look at our parents. I am never binding myself to anyone or taking a mate."

"The bond isn't important. Saving Ambrose is." Nyx glanced between them. "Will you help me or not?"

Niamh sighed. "Do we have a choice?"

"Of course, but I'd be happier to have you two to back me up."

"I don't want to go." Novia shook her head. "Why should we risk our lives for the man who is responsible for us dying?"

"I agree with her. We're not risking ourselves for him. Besides, the queen is a much more pressing issue," Niamh said.

"We can't stop her without Ambrose." Nyx slumped back in her seat, defeated.

Part of her could understand her sisters' reluctance, but she didn't want to leave Ambrose to a fate worse than death.

The Archdruid wouldn't kill him. Not until he destroyed every part of him. That was how the Archdruid worked.

"Maybe we should cast the death spell again," Nyx suggested. "See what else we can remember?"

Niamh shook her head. "That won't change anything."

"It would help us remember more. Maybe we can find the location of the shield."

"It's worth a try. Let's do it."

Novia rose. "Forgive me if I don't want to die again. It's late. We should all get some sleep."

Nyx climbed into bed beside Darius to find he'd already fallen asleep. She slumped back against the soft pillows. Unable to sleep. Why couldn't her sisters agree to help? Even Darius seemed reluctant to go back. But she knew he wanted to.

She lay there and chanted a spell to mimic death.

Darkness dragged her under. This time, she found herself huddled in a large chamber with ivory stone walls. Her sisters stood beside her.

"Mama, what's happening?" she asked Evony.

"My queen, the Archdruid is attacking. We must flee." Lyra appeared near the altar.

Evony paced up and down. "I am not fleeing from my own realm."

"It's alright," she whispered to her sisters. "Mama won't let anything happen to us."

Niamh scrunched up her face. "Why won't Mama stop this? Where is Papa?"

"He left us," Novia whispered.

"Mama, do something." Nyx clenched her tiny fists.

"Quiet, Aerin. I must think." Her mother's voice lashed against her like a whip.

"Quieten down, girls." Velestra knelt in front of them.

"Here, drink this."

Three sisters ignored her.

"Where are my guards? Where is my damned husband?" Evony demanded.

"Girls, you must drink this." Velestra held out the flask. "Please."

Nyx shook her head. "We're not thirsty."

Evony and Lyra continued arguing.

"This potion will keep you safe. Please, just drink it." Velestra shoved the flask to Nyx. *Drink it. It's the only way to keep you and your sisters alive.*

Nyx hesitated. *What is it?*

It's to protect you. Drink up.

She gulped down the foul brew and her sisters did the same. A few moments later, the temple's doors burst open.

Nyx opened her eyes and found herself back in bed.

Velestra gave them something. She must have known who they were when she met Nyx and Niamh a few months ago. Yet she said nothing. She had to find out why.

Nyx raised her hand and muttered a sleeping spell to ensure he wouldn't wake up. He flinched but didn't stir. She slipped out of bed, then transported outside.

Scanning the palace, she sensed her sisters and the others were already asleep. Good. It was better if no one followed her.

"Ember?" Nyx called.

The black dragon and Sirin flew down to greet her.

"Sirin, you can't be here. I don't want Darius to know I'm leaving."

Why not?

Because I need to see someone alone. And it's safer if he stays here. So make sure he stays.

He'll follow you.

She sighed. "I know, but if he can't get through the

shield, then he won't be able to follow me."

I could take you, Sirin offered.

She shook her head. "You will be recognised. I need a dragon to blend in." She scrambled onto Ember's back.

What if you get into trouble? None of us —

I'll be fine. Don't worry. Just keep Darius and the others safe. She turned to Baron and Andre as they flew over to join them. *Make sure my sisters don't follow me. They won't be happy when they find out I'm gone.*

It's not safe, Baron protested.

I should go with you, Sirin insisted. *And Darius, too. What if the Archdruid finds you?*

Just keep everyone safe.

I'll protect her. Ember spread his wings and took off.

One way or another, she would find out what Velestra had done.

Ember could fly even faster than Sirin. She still felt strange about her connection to the dragon.

Ember, how did you end up in the Dragon Guard?

We woke up in the tomb and you and your sisters were gone. Someone found us and handed us to the Dragon Guard.

Didn't you search for us?

I didn't know where to look. I couldn't sense you anymore. I hoped you'd come back. Ember swooped low until they reached a spot where the shield was.

Nyx tapped Ambrose's staff on the ground. The shield flashed into existence but didn't open.

"Open, damn it."

Nothing.

It won't open, Ember remarked.

"Azura?" Nyx called.

After a few moments, the mermaid surfaced.

"What do you want?" Azura asked.

"I need your help. I need you to get us through the shield."

Azura snorted. "I can't get through it. We've only ever left when the queen allowed us to."

"I think with your help and Dahlia's, we should be able to get through. Please, I have to get to Ambrose. Will you help or not?"

"Will you stop the queen?"

"I'll damn well try."

"Good, let's go." Azura swam ahead of them. "I'll show the spot where the queen used to send us through."

Nyx strapped the staff to her back and held on to Ember. Ember didn't have any trouble keeping up with the mermaid.

"This is it." Azura stopped along the side of the riverbank. "I could see through here and hear people. The rest of the shield doesn't allow tat."

"The shield must be thinner here." Nyx raised the staff. "Open." Light flashed, but the shield didn't budge. "Argh, why won't it do as I command?" She reached out to touch the shield and static charged against her fingers.

"Why won't it open?" Azura pushed against it. "Ambrose always used his staff to come through."

"Maybe if you join powers with me, it might allow the shield to open."

Azura reached up and took Nyx's hand.

Light flashed as the death fae appeared. "Something is wrong with Taliesin. Az, you need to come. I think the queen has possessed him."

Nyx sighed. "Of course, my mother would go to the only immortal she could find. You should stay away from Taliesin. If the queen has him, she'll turn her sights on you. Dahlia, can you touch the shield? I need to get through. Maybe since your power is like death, you won't be affected by the barrier."

Dahlia reached out and all three women screamed as they fell into the river on the other side.

Ember flew into the air to keep Nyx airborne.

"We are through," Azura gasped. "This is so —"

"Quiet, there's probably Dragon Guards nearby," Nyx hissed. "Dahlia, you weren't meant to come through."

Dahlia climbed onto the dragon. "Well, I'm here. Where are we headed? To save Ambrose?"

"That's the plan. I have to make a quick stop first."

"Good, I'm coming with you. Trust me, you'll need my help."

Azura stared up at them. "I'll stay close by and be ready for when you bring Ambrose back. What about your sisters?"

"It's safer if they stay inside the shield. Ember, let's go."

Dahlia didn't hold on to her.

Are you sure the death fae isn't your mother? Ember asked.

She is not. Her power deflects all magic. Even mine.

I still don't like her. Ilari are very dangerous.

She helped us get through, and she cared for Ambrose. He did a lot to help her and the other Outsiders. Nyx glanced back at the shield. *No turning back now.*

Ember flew over Varden Forest as they headed towards the Varden's village. They landed near the huts.

"Dragon!" someone yelled.

Ember, you need to shift. The people here don't like dragons.

Light shimmered around the dragon as Ember shifted into a large black wolf.

Nyx and Dahlia hit the ground hard.

Ember growled as several Varden riders surrounded them.

"Hold your fire. We didn't come here to harm anyone."

Nyx raised her hands in surrender.

"You have a dragon," one man said.

"Do you see any dragons here? No." She motioned around them.

"Death fae," another rider spat.

Dahlia smirked. "I'd put your weapons down if I were you."

"I'm here to see Velestra. She knows me. Besides, I'm the Morrigan's daughter. So move aside."

To her surprise, the riders lowered their weapons. "The Morrigan has returned?" one rider asked.

"Returned? She never left."

"Where is she?"

"Never mind. Where's Velestra?"

"I'm here." Velestra stepped forward. "Nyx, what are you doing here?"

"You lied to me. You said you didn't know who I was. Why?"

"Because I followed her orders." Velestra fired her staff and a blast of light shot towards Nyx.

Dahlia stepped in front of her and winced as the blast hit her tattooed skin. "That tingles."

"Velestra, what are you doing? I'm Nyx — I mean, Aerin. You used to be my guard."

She's been touched by a mind whisperer, Ember said. *Her soul is no longer her own.*

Wonderful. How do I free her?

Only your mother can do that or death.

Dahlia, can you kill her and bring her back? Nyx asked. *It might be the only way to save her and release her from my mother's hold.*

I can try. Are you sure it will free her? I thought the person who was touched by a mind whisperer could only be freed by the one who used their power to run them.

"Just do it."

Dahlia raised her hand and smoke billowed around Velestra. Velestra slumped to the ground. Dahlia bent over her and blew some white smoke into Velestra's mouth.

The other fae gasped and sat up. "What's going on?" She seemed dazed.

"Is she free?" Dahlia arched an eyebrow.

"Maybe. Velestra, how do you feel?" Nyx went over to her.

"Strange. Was I…"

"Dead? Yes." Dahlia nodded. "Is she under the queen's control?"

Nyx scanned the other fae with her mind. "I don't think so. Her mind is clear now."

"Was I under the queen's control?" Velestra furrowed her brow. "Oh gods, the queen. She is back."

"She never really left." Nyx shook her head. "I'm sorry Dahlia had to kill you, but it's the only way to free you."

"I don't understand. Why would the queen do that?"

"Because she likes to control everyone around her." Nyx gave her a hand up. "Why didn't you tell me you used to be my guard?"

"You remember that?"

"A little. What did you give me and my sisters to drink that day in the temple?"

"A potion to protect you from death. It put you into a healing sleep, but after the execution none of you would wake." Velestra touched Nyx's cheek. "I still don't know how you came back after so long."

"I have a good idea about that. Thanks for what you did. My sisters and I owe you."

"I was just doing my duty. Besides, you were my girls. I loved all of you. I wouldn't let you die."

"Where did you get the potion?"

"From your grandmother."

Her eyes widened. "The Great Guardian never interferes."

"Perhaps she made an exception."

"Nyx, we need to go." Dahlia tapped her foot. "Or we'll lose the cover of darkness."

She had a point.

"Ember, change back into a dragon."

Ember shifted back into dragon form.

"Where are you going?" Velestra asked.

Nyx opened her mouth and hesitated. "It's safer if you don't know." She scrambled onto the dragon. Dahlia climbed on after her.

"Wait, if you need help, let me and the other riders assist you." Velestra put a hand on Ember.

"I can't ask you to put your lives at risk. And you can't come with us.

"We all swore to protect the queen and her family. That hasn't changed."

"Protect the old city." Nyx urged Ember on and flew away from the forest.

CHAPTER 28

Darius.

The sound of someone calling his name dragged him from the depths of sleep.

Darius!

He opened his eyes and reached out for Nyx only to find the bed empty.

"Nyx?" He sat up and cast his senses out but he couldn't detect her presence. Holy spirits, where had she gone?

Darius, Nyx is gone. Sirin's voice rang through his mind.

I can see that. Where is she?

She flew off with Ember.

When? He scrambled out of bed.

About an hour ago. She asked me not to tell you but I'm worried.

"Of course she did." He pulled on a shirt and yanked his other clothes on.

She's gone to rescue Ambrose.

I'll have to go after her. Darius couldn't believe she had gone off on a suicide mission. Darius wanted Ambrose back too but he knew the risks. *Why didn't you wake me earlier?*

I tried but I couldn't wake up.

No doubt Nyx used magic on me. Sirin, be ready to leave.

Darius hurried down the hall to Niamh's chamber. He didn't bother knocking and went through her. "Niamh, wake up." He shook her shoulder.

Niamh bolted up and shoved the dagger under his throat. Her long blond hair fell over her face.

He raised a hand to stop her. "It's me. Put that thing away. Nyx has gone after Ambrose."

She lowered the dagger and shoved her hair off her face. "What? When?"

"At least an hour ago and she spelled me so I wouldn't sense it."

Niamh leapt out of bed. "I can't believe she —"

"I should have known she'd do something like this."

"Well, let's go and get her back."

Darius headed out and knocked on Ranelle and Lucien's doors. "Nyx is gone. We need to find her."

Something shattered the air and the palace walls trembled.

"What was that?" Niamh came out of her room fully dressed and armed.

Darius touched the screen and a hologram of the city formed.

"The shield is failing," the keeper announced.

"Holy spirits, some of the Dragon Guard are close by." Darius went to the window.

"What?" Niamh joined him. "How did they get here? The shield —"

"The shield is failing faster than we thought," Darius remarked. "In a few hours it will be completely down."

Novia came out. "The Dragon Guard — what should we do?"

Niamh turned to Darius. "We'll go out and fight them. Can you stop them like you did the other dragons?"

"I don't know if I can bring all the dragons down. No doubt my father will have found a way around that." Everything in him screamed at him to go and find Nyx. But

213

he wouldn't leave the others high and dry. "If they got through, a whole battalion could be here." He grimaced.

"If they're coming here, you can go and get Nyx back. We need her, too. She is the strongest of the three of us."

"I can't leave —"

"Go. We'll hold things down here until you and Nyx get back."

"But —"

"Go, Darius," Lucien insisted. "We can handle a few Dragon Guards."

"Alright, I'll be back as soon as I can."

Darius hurried outside and climbed onto Sirin's back. He activated all of her runes to cloak and shield them. *We've got to get to Nyx,* he told his dragon.

But what about the Dragon Guard?

Darius reached out to the other dragons with his mind and commanded them to stop. A wall of resistance met him. He blew out a breath. *My father has put mental blocks on them all. My power won't work. Maybe there's something else I can do.*

He raised his hand and Zephyr the spirit appeared. Zephyr was an underling that he sometimes used when he needed help. "Master, how may I serve you?"

"Zephyr, get as many spirits as you can and stop the Dragon Guard. Try to force them to leave. But don't harm them unless you have to," he warned. "Do not take on anyone but my father's forces."

Sirin took to the air and shadows shot up alongside them.

Sirin roared in discomfort. *Are you sure that's wise? They could kill them.*

The Dragon Guard are well trained and powerful.

You will have their blood on your hands.

Darius winced. *I told z*

214

Zephyr not to kill them. Plus, my father knows I will use sorcery. He will be prepared for that. At least the spirits might be able to slow them down for a while. He didn't want to kill anyone but if they didn't fight back they'd all die.

He opened a portal once they were outside the fractured shield.

A few moments later, they reappeared near Alaris.

Darius cast his senses out but couldn't detect her there either. *Damn, where is she?*

Nyx? he called out for her.

No reply came.

I can't sense her either, Sirin remarked. *Or Ember.*

Head for the palace.

Soon the glowing dome of the Crystal Palace loomed ahead of them.

How are we going to get in? The guards will recognise you.

I know a way in. Head straight for the dome.

The dome? But —

Trust me. I know the palace better than my father.

Fergus spent months away from the palace so Darius knew some entrances wouldn't be covered.

As they drew closer, Darius twisted the bracelet he found in the queen's vault. Light flared all over his body as he transformed.

Once they reached the dome he dropped onto it.

Sirin, find somewhere close by to hide. Be ready for my call.

Be careful. You and Nyx better come out of there alive. Sirin vanished into the distance.

Gideon's face stared back at him in the shining dome. It felt odd to look like his brother. But who else would be better to help him get around undetected?

Darius hoped the device would cloak him and his magic. Fumbling around, he opened the dome and slid inside.

Most people didn't know the palace's secret passages. Darius had discovered it by accident when he was a child.

His father only used the known passages. Darius suspected the palace builders put in the other and kept them a secret from Fergus. He kept his senses alert and only scanned the palace once. Or else his parents might sense him.

Nyx, where are you? he called for her again.

She didn't respond. Either she couldn't do so or she had ignored him.

Nyx, please answer me. Darius sighed and headed down spiral steps. Cobwebs covered the stairwell. His mind raced as he planned out his next move.

Gideon was already at the palace so he'd have to be careful not to run into his brother.

When he reached the bottom of the stairwell he hesitated. How could he find Nyx if he couldn't sense her? If he couldn't find her, he could at least search for Ambrose himself.

Darius pressed his hand to the wall and its lid open. The hallway appeared empty. The wall slid back into place after he climbed through.

Nyx? he called for her again.

Still nothing.

Darius straightened. To pull this off he'd have to act like his brother and have his smug air of confidence. As he rounded the corner, guards barred his way.

"Stand aside," he snapped in Gideon's voice.

"Sorry, milord. We are under orders not to let anyone roam around. Aren't you supposed to be confined to your chambers?"

Darius punched the guard in the face. Just as he is brother would do. "How dare you question your prince."

He growled. "Has anyone been captured breaking into the palace?" He had to know if Nyx had already been caught.

The guard yelped and clutched his bloody nose.

The other guard answered, "No one, my lord."

"Do you know where my father took Ambrose?" Gideon wouldn't be privy to that information. The guards glanced at each other.

"Only the Archdruid knows that."

CHAPTER 29

"How are we going to get into the palace?" Dahlia wanted to know. "Do you want me to kill the guards?"

Nyx shook her head. "I know a way in. So we can get into the palace undetected. The hardest part will be finding Ambrose."

"Can't you sense him?"

"He's probably somewhere shielded. I just hope he's still in the palace. I feel his presence there, but it's faint."

Darius's knowledge of the secret passages would come in handy. *Ember, drop us on top of the dome. Can you shift into something small?*

Of course.

Once they got near the dome, she grabbed Dahlia's arm and jumped. Images flashed before her eyes.

More memories? Dahlia asked.

She nodded. *I don't know why I have to be close to death to remember my old life.*

Maybe because you were in the state between life and death.

Maybe.

Ember shifted into a small wolf and headed through the open passage.

Ember, try and sniff out Ambrose.

How can your dragon change shape? Dahlia frowned. *What is he?*

He's a long story. She followed in after him. Dahlia slid in behind her and closed the door. Nyx kept her senses on alert as she headed down the narrow stairway. *Can you see in the dark?*

Not really.

Raising her hand, she conjured a small green orb over Dahlia. Nyx didn't need it as her eyes adjusted to the darkness and made it appear like midday.

Ambrose's presence hovered somewhere in the palace, but something blocked her from getting an exact location on him. That didn't surprise her. So much dark magic filled the Crystal Palace that it always made it hard to sense things here. Calling him in thought wouldn't help either.

What's the plan when we do find Ambrose? Dahlia asked.

At this point, there is no plan. We just have to find him. I should be able to transport us out. If not, we'll use this route. We have guards and a strange creature to deal with. I do have these. She handed Dahlia a bracelet. *These are glamour devices. They can transform you to look and sound like someone else. We should be able to disguise ourselves.* She twisted hers. Her wings retracted into her body. Her hair became shorter and dark brown. Her skin darker.

"I look like Elise. A guard who works here. You look like a servant."

Dahlia's hair turned red and her skin freckled. "This is strange." Dahlia touched her face, and her voice sounded different.

"Agreed. Pretend like you know the place. I know these two from my visits to the palace. They are always gossiping together." She stopped at the end of the stairwell and took a deep breath. *Ember, change into a dog. We need to blend in. I know Elise feeds strays.*

Ember shifted again.

Ready?

219

Both fae and canine nodded.

She waved her hand so a mop and bucket appeared. Nyx touched the wall, and the panel slid open. The way beyond lay empty. The wall slid shut again as they emerged.

Ambrose is somewhere on this floor. Let's go.

When she opened a set of double doors, guards blocked their way. She hadn't expected to encounter them so soon.

"What are you doing up here?" the guard demanded.

"Just came to clean on this floor. Housekeeper will have my head if I don't."

Thank the gods she had listened to Ada's thoughts and learnt as much as she could about how the palace worked.

The guard narrowed his eyes. "Why are you up here, Imogen?"

"Off shift now. With that creature up here, I figured I'd better keep an eye on my best mate." Dahlia easily slipped into her character.

The guard shuddered. "You're right about that. The blood sucker gives me the shivers."

Blood sucker? What kind of creature do they have up here? Dahlia asked.

I don't know. Darius had never seen it before.

She almost sighed with relief when the guard let them through.

"Why do you have a dog with you?" the second guard asked.

"He's harmless. He follows me everywhere."

She and Ember headed into one of the chambers while Dahlia stayed in the hall. *Nyx, there's something here.*

She put her bucket and mop down, then headed out. At least the guards were on the other end of the hall.

Ambrose is here. I can feel him, Dahlia added.

"Hey, what are you two —" the first guard called out.

Dahlia raised her hand and blew tendrils of smoke at them. Both guards collapsed. She and Nyx dragged them into the empty room.

Nyx's senses prickled. But it didn't matter. Nothing was going to stop her from saving her father.

Ready?

Dahlia nodded.

Ember stuck close to her as she opened the door.

A dark-haired woman stood by the window. She whirled around to face them. Her eyes burned red and her fangs bared.

"Gods, she's one of the damned." Dahlia gasped.

"I'm here to clean up. The housekeeper —" Nyx didn't let her fear show but her heart pounded.

"Liar. You really think you can hide your presence, mind whisperer?" The woman turned to Dahlia. "Death fae."

She lunged towards Nyx. Nyx raised her hand and her power rippled against the creature.

The damned. This was what a mind whisperer became if they gave into the dark side of their power and lost their soul.

My touch won't work on her! Nyx cried and dodged the woman when she made a grab for Nyx.

Too bad her knowledge didn't tell her how to kill one of the damned.

Dahlia grabbed the woman's arm. "Maybe mine will. Get Ambrose." She punched the woman in the face.

Nyx winced at the crunch of bone and cartilage. "Ambrose?" She rushed over to the bed.

Ambrose's eyes were closed, and he lay unmoving. When she touched him, a web of energy glowed over his body. It repelled her touch.

Move. She called on her magic and willed it to move his body. Green orbs sparkled around him, but he remained rooted in place.

Ember shifted back into a dragon and shot fire at the damned woman. The creature dodged it and advanced towards Dahlia again. She knocked the Ilari across the room and lunged towards Nyx.

Nyx yelped as the woman's talons dug into her throat. *Fire kills the damned,* Ember said.

"Shoot fire at Ambrose." She motioned towards the bed. *But what if —?*

Do it!

Ember shot a column of fire at the druid, and the web around him exploded. He turned towards the damned woman. She screamed as she burst into flame in an explosion of fiery light.

"Help me get him up." She yanked Ambrose up and he slumped onto Ember's back. "Ambrose, wake up." She shook his shoulder.

"Forget that. Let's go." Dahlia scrambled up.

Light flashed as Fergus himself appeared. "Where do you think you're going with my prisoner?"

Ember hurled a blast of fire at the Archdruid. Fergus waved the flames away, then raised his hands. Power pulsed through the air and pounded against Nyx like a heavy drum. She'd been on the receiving end of his power before. This time felt much worse. She didn't have Darius' magic anymore, either.

Dahlia screamed and clutched her head. Even an Ilari wasn't immune from the Archdruid's power.

No! Nyx slammed her mental shield in place. Now she knew there'd be no getting out of this. She crawled across the floor, her limbs like heavy weights under the strain of the Archdruid's power. Raising her hand, Ember, Dahlia and Ambrose vanished in a flash of green orbs.

CHAPTER 30

Darius gasped when he reached the bottom of the staircase. Pain tore through him. "Argh, Nyx." His father had her. He'd arrived too late, but it didn't matter. He had to get to her fast. He shoved the panel open and climbed out. It closed behind him.

His mind raced. How long had Fergus had Nyx? What would he do to her? Darius pushed those thoughts away.

Two guards barred his way when he got to the room where Ambrose was being held.

"Sorry, milord. You can't go through. We're under strict orders from the Archdruid." The first guard held an arm out to stop him.

"I want to see the prisoner."

"My lord, the prisoner is gone. That fae girl sent him away." The second guard rubbed the back of his neck. "Damn that death fae knocked me out. My head still hurts."

"What death fae? What girl?" Darius demanded.

"A mind whisperer and a death fac came. The mind whisperer made the prisoner disappear. Your father sent the Dragon Guard to bring him back."

"Where are the mind whisperer and the death fae?"

"The death fae escaped with the druid. The Archdruid has the girl locked up."

Darius shoved past them and headed straight into Ambrose's chamber. Scorch marks covered the wall. Dragon fire. He'd know that anywhere.

"My lord, you can't be in here." The guard came in behind him. "You must leave."

He felt Nyx's magic here too, but he couldn't sense her presence. "Where did he take the prisoner? That mind whisperer was involved with my mother's death. I want to know where she is." He grabbed the guard by his tunic.

"We — we don't know. The Archdruid took her away. You should know your father —"

He shoved the guard aside and stormed out.

Would his father have taken Nyx somewhere else or kept her here? He doubted the Archdruid would kill her straight away. Fergus would want to question her first. Fergus wouldn't use the dungeons to house such a valuable prisoner. So where would he go? Glenfel? That would be an ideal place since Fergus could transport onto the island.

But the vault was here, too. A place that existed outside time and place. Fergus kept his collection of records, weapons and treasures there. It would be an ideal place to hide a prisoner. He wouldn't be able to sense Nyx there either.

Hurrying down the hall, he made his way to where the vault door was located. Darius almost doubled over as pain tore through him. No, not his pain — Nyx's.

Gritting his teeth, he touched the crystals and put in the vault's combination to open the door. Nothing happened. His father had changed the sequence since Darius had last been there a couple of months ago.

The last time he'd been here, he'd had Nyx with him. She managed to use her powers to learn the combination. Maybe the link between them worked both ways. Maybe he could tap into her powers.

225

Closing his eyes, he touched one of the crystals. Nothing happened, more pain shot through him. Lightning flared between his fingers as he blasted crystals. Each one exploded, sending shards flying.

The vault's door flashed into existence.

"Rombus." He used sorcery and threw a lightning bolt at the same time. Sorcery and druid magic made a powerful combination. The door shattered as he entered the vault.

It looked as he remembered. Floor-to-ceiling covered in books, scrolls and crystals and weapons. Two druidon guards stood there with staff weapons at the ready. That meant his father had to be here.

One fired a staff at him.

Darius waved the blast of energy away as he drew more magic. To overcome his father, he would need to use all the power at his disposal. He fired two bolts of lightning at them. Both druidons dodged his magic.

Calling up more power so his body became enveloped with lightning, bolts shot in every direction. Lightning flashed around the shelves. His father would never allow anyone to destroy his precious possessions.

Both guards exploded in a blast of fire.

He blew out a breath and hurried through, searching the rest of the vault. But he found no one.

Where was Nyx and his father? They had to be here somewhere. Yet the vault looked the same. His father always left everything meticulous and liked everything in order.

Nyx? he called her with his mind.

She didn't respond, but she had to be here somewhere.

Darius stopped in the middle of the room. If he could feel her, he could find her.

Nyx, where are you? He went over to the far wall where a shelf stood covered in crystals. He'd never paid much attention to it since he always came to use his father's books.

Pushing against the shelf, the wall vanished. Hurrying through the opening, he turned the corner and found Nyx crumpled on the ground.

His father stood a few feet away, hand outstretched. "I wondered when you'd turn up, boy. Come to save your precious mind whisperer, have you?"

Darius dropped the facade and twisted the bracelet. Light flashed as he transformed back into himself. "Father, you don't need to hurt her. She's not a threat to you."

"She's a mind whisperer and shouldn't be alive. I can't believe my own son would fall victim to the likes of her."

"I didn't fall victim to Nyx. She's not the queen. If you want the queen, she's on the loose in the old city." He didn't care if his father found the queen now. Keeping the queen captive was no longer his priority.

"Oh, I'll get the queen soon enough. That Andovian wench won't escape me again."

Darius hit him with a lightning bolt.

Fergus caught the lightning between his fingers. "You'll have to do better than that, boy. A little lightning won't hurt me."

He called up his full power again. Bolts of light shot from his hands.

Nyx was gone. He could feel it. Something inside him snapped. He blasted his father against the wall. Then hurried over to Nyx. Touching her, he couldn't find a pulse.

Fergus shot to his feet and white fire crackled between his fingers, then he threw a fireball straight at Darius.

Picking Nyx up, he dodged the fireball. He chanted a spell to transport out and light flashed around them as they reappeared outside the entrance to the dome passageway.

Too bad he couldn't transfer out of the palace, but he didn't want his father tracking his magic.

Sliding into the passage, he checked Nyx's pulse again, but found none.

Why would his father kill her so quickly? Wouldn't he have questioned and tortured her first?

It didn't matter. All that mattered was getting back to the old city.

One way or another, he'd find a way to bring her back.

Sirin, I need you. Be ready to come and get us.

On my way.

Darius winced as the weight of her body dragged him down. He clutched her close to him as he ascended. It seemed to take forever to reach the final step. Below, guards banged against the walls as they searched for the passage entrance.

Darius shoved the dome's panel open. Cold night air stung his face.

Where was Sirin? She should be back by now.

Sirin, where are you?

I'm coming, but there are guards everywhere.

A large black mass leapt on top of the dome.

Ember.

Nyx? The dragon whimpered.

"She is —" He couldn't bring himself to say it, let alone think it. "Never mind. How are you here? I thought your life force was tied to hers?"

I feared something would happen to her, so I pulled power from you through your bond to her. It's the only thing keeping me alive.

"Get us out of here." He scrambled onto the dragon's back.

Ember took off. *The old city has fallen. There are Dragon Guards everywhere.*

What about the palace?

It's still warded, but both of her sisters are dead.

What? How?

I don't know. They fell in the middle of battle. When I felt Nyx die, they died too. So are Andre and Baron.

She and her sisters are linked by magic. There must be a way to bring them back. I've done it before.

That was different. They took a potion to put them in the healing sleep before.

Blasts of fire came at them as more dragons came closer.

Head for the Spirit Grove.

A web of glowing light filled up the night sky as the Archdruid appeared on top of the palace's roof. Ember screamed as the web of energy wrapped around him and Darius, pulling them back towards the palace.

Darius knew he was trapped now.

CHAPTER 31

Nyx found herself surrounded by light. All the pain from the Archdruid's torture faded. Images flashed around her of playing with her sisters. Days with their father and gruelling lessons with their mother.

Memories came back up until the point of being hit by the Archdruid's staff weapon. Her eyes fluttered open. It took a few moments for her to come back to herself. She was Aerin. But she was still Nyx Ashwood.

A cuff now encircled her wrist — the guards had slapped it on her when she had been captured. It took her a moment to remember where she was. The Archdruid's cell.

Darius lay a few feet away, unmoving.

The Archdruid had left now a dark-haired woman came in. Another one of the damned.

"You murdered my sister." The woman gave her a cold stare.

"Oh, you must mean the damned woman who guarded Ambrose. Your sister hurt my father, so I guess we're even."

"I'll drain you both dry."

Nyx raised her hand and fire shot from her fingers. The woman exploded in a burst of flame.

The cuff fell off her wrist. Odd. Why would it come off? It should have rendered her powerless, but it didn't matter.

Then she remembered Darius had said something about his cuff coming off when he had come close to death.

She stared at her hands. Where did the fire come from? It wasn't part of her magic. No… It had been part of her magic. Back when she had been Aerin. All druids had an affinity for a different element. It seemed hers had been fire.

She crawled over to Darius and pressed her ear to his chest. "Druid?" She still heard his heart beating, at least. "Druid, wake up." Her hand came away bloody when she touched his chest.

The cell door creaked open and Gideon came in. "Well, well, look what we have here. I knew I'd catch both of you."

She scowled at him. "You didn't. Your father did."

"Yes, but you're still trapped. So tell me, mind whisperer, who killed my mother? Was it you? I should have known the Andovian Queen had control of my brother."

That sounded so ridiculous, she laughed. "I'm not the queen, you fool. She killed your mother, not me."

"And you expect me to believe that? You're a liar. I've known that from the moment I laid eyes on you." He raised his hand, then the cuff encircled her wrist again.

Damn it, why hadn't she used her power to get them out of there when she had the chance?

Gideon yanked her up by her hair. "I will kill you. But first you will suffer the way my mother did." She yelped and punched him so hard his head reeled back. It loosened his grip, so she used her other hand to punch him again. He dropped like a stone.

The fool had left the cell door unlocked, so she shoved it open, put the cuff on Gideon and dragged Darius out. She slammed the door shut and locked it.

Nyx sagged under the weight of his body. She had to get them out of there. Transporting out of the prison wouldn't be an option.

"Stop!" a guard yelled as he rounded the corner.

Not a Dragon Guard, since his thoughts buzz through her mind. All the Dragon Guard had strong mental shields.

Fatigue weighed on her like a heavy cloak. She grabbed the man's arm and power jolted between them and shook the air like thunder. She sank to her knees beside Darius.

"Are you hurt?" The guard bent and put a hand on her shoulder.

"Help my druid up."

The guard yanked Darius up.

Nyx's head spun. "You have to get us out of here and protect us both. We need to hurry. One of the secret passages would be the quickest way out of the palace."

"Palace?" The guard furrowed his brow. "We are not in the palace."

Her mouth fell open. "What? Where are we?"

"Morden Tower on the North-East island of Andovia."

North-east island. Where the Archdruid interrogated prisoners. Like Glenfel, it was shielded by magic. Darius had told her about the place.

She wouldn't be able to get off the island either.

"Only the Archdruid can transport off the island," the guard added. "Even if you escape the tower, you can't leave."

Darius groaned as he came awake. "Nyx?"

"Druid." She grinned. "What happened?"

"My father overpowered me. I thought you were —"

"I was. Well, for a few moments at most." She put her arm under him for support. "Guard, go on ahead. We have to get out of here."

"We are in Morden Tower." Darius winced.

"Yes, how do we get out?"

"We can't. Only my father can use magic to transport on and off the island."

"Why can't you channel his power? You have done it before."

"Because I'm weak, but there might be a way if you can help me."

"I'm not sure either of us are up to using magic right now."

"Why do images keep flashing through my mind?" He clutched his head.

"Probably my memories. I guess our bond is allowing you to access them."

"The Archdruid is back," the guard called out.

"We need a way out of here."

Runes. Those runes you use — they are older than my father's magic.

"Are there any rooms around here or somewhere we could hide?" Nyx asked the guard.

"This way." The guard led them to a storeroom that had cleaning supplies in it.

"Go back to your post, but do not tell anyone about us." The guard nodded, and Nyx closed the door. She knelt on the floor beside Darius. She bit her finger hard enough to draw blood.

She and Darius traced runes together, but nothing happened.

"The guard won't stand a chance. You can move quicker without me." Darius leaned back against the wall.

She shook her head. "I can't leave you. I won't."

"But —"

"I'm not leaving you. I never will, so forget about it."

"My father will kill you. If you can escape, you can get back to your sisters." He clutched her hand. "I can't watch you die."

"I won't let you die either." She held back tears and wrapped her arms around him. "We're staying together. No matter what."

Darius wrapped an arm around her. "I love you."

She wiped her tears away. "I love you too." She kissed him, then rested her head against his chest.

If they died soon, at least they would be together. She thought about her grove — the place she always went into in her mind when things felt hopeless. With its towering trees and feeling of comfort. It had always been her safe place.

Light flashed around them as their runes flared to life.

They reappeared in the grove — her grove.

"How is this possible?" Nyx pulled away from him and gasped. "This place isn't real." The heady scent of leaves in the wind filled her nostrils. She bent and picked up a leaf. "Is it? It feels…"

"Like a forest?" The Great Guardian appeared. "That's because it is. This is where the tree of souls and the Spirit Grove exist." Her long raven hair fell to her waist, her ivory skin shimmered like moonlight, and her blue eyes held centuries of wisdom. She wore a lilac silk robe that she might like cobwebs covered in dew.

Nyx furrowed her brow. "You taught me about this place."

The Guardian smiled. "You remember. Death would have erased the magic I used to make you forget."

"I don't understand. How did we get here?" Darius clutched his abdomen. "No one gets out of that tower."

The Great Guardian's smile widened. "Love is the greatest of all magics and the most powerful."

"He needs help." Nyx wrapped an arm around him. "Come. You can both rest here."

"What about the Archdruid?"

"He can't enter here. He's not welcome." The Great Guardian held her hand over Darius's chest and the wound closed over.

"I thought you didn't interfere?" Darius furrowed his brow.

"I don't." The Guardian shook her head. "But sometimes I make an exception. Especially when the Archdruid is wreaking havoc."

"You're the one who gave Velestra that potion." Nyx crossed her arms and glared at her grandmother.

"What potion?" Darius glanced between them.

"Velestra gave me and my sisters a potion that put us to sleep before your father shot us. I still don't know what it was."

Surprise flashed over the guardian's face. "It was meant to put the three of you into a healing sleep."

"Why did we stay dead for almost a century?"

"Because the potion didn't have time to take full effect."

"So we were dead?"

The Guardian shook her head again. "You were in a state between life and death. At least until Darius brought you back."

"Did you have something to do with it?" Darius took Nyx's hand.

"No, Evony did. That wasn't my doing. After Ambrose found out you three had come back, I sent you out of Andovia. I erased your memories so you could start normal lives."

"Why would you split us up? We're sisters! We belong together." Her fists clenched.

"If you stayed together, you would have been discovered sooner."

"So you had someone sell us as slaves then?" Nyx couldn't believe the Guardian — someone she'd trusted — could have done such a thing.

"That wasn't meant to happen. You were supposed to be safe, but I had no control over what happened to you after you left Andovia."

"You could have saved us. Our parents were alive."

"Nyx —"

"Don't. You've said enough already." Nyx stormed off before the Guardian could say another word.

CHAPTER 32

Novia's heart pounded in her ears as she and her sister stood around the well with Lucien. She couldn't believe the queen had escaped. The very thing she had been terrified of.

Now Nyx had run off to save Ambrose and left them on their own. In a few hours, the shield would be completely down. Some of the Outsiders had already come seeking sanctuary at the palace.

"What should we do with Lyra's body?" Novia whispered to her sister.

"See if we can revive her and maybe she can help. The palace's wards aren't going to protect us for long." Niamh shrugged. "If not, make sure the queen can't use her again. I called Azura and asked her to come and help," Niamh added. "If Lyra's soul is still in there, she's going to need a lot of healing."

"How could her soul still be in there?" Novia gaped at her. "Wouldn't the queen have — removed of her somehow?"

"Azura said the queen released Lyra twenty years ago. So Lyra's soul could still be in there." Niamh grimaced. "Probably repressed."

Lucien jumped into the well and soon emerged, carrying Lyra's body. The former priestess' skin had turned grey and hollow. "She has no pulse," Lucien told them. "You can't heal her."

Ranelle knelt and touched Lyra's forehead. "Her spirit is still in there. It's faint but there."

Azura and Bones appeared. "Holy spirits," Azura swore and put her hand over her mouth.

"We thought you'd want a chance to say goodbye to her." Niamh touched Azura's shoulder. "We can probably help her to move on —"

"No." Azura shook her head. "I can heal her."

"Azura, you can't heal a corpse. Her body is too weak," Bones said.

The pirate had a point. Surely Azura couldn't expect to save Lyra? Her body was beyond the point of saving.

"I'm not losing her again." Azura knelt and held her hands over her mother, bathing the body in bright white light.

Shouldn't we do something to stop her? Novia glanced around at the others.

It's her mother. She is going to want to save her, Niamh pointed out.

"Azura." Bones stepped forward. "You can't save her. Let her so move on so she can be at peace."

"The queen took her life away. Why shouldn't she have it back?" Azura snapped.

"If her soul moves on, we can burn her body so the queen can never use it again," Niamh said.

"I won't let her die." Azura bared her teeth.

"This is a part of life. It's not an end but a beginning — Dahlia always says that." Bones knelt beside her. "You know this. The people we love never really leave us."

A tear dripped down Azura's cheek.

Light flared over Lyra's body and the priestess' eyes flew open. "Where — where am I? Lyra rasped, dazed.

"How did you do that?" Niamh gaped at her friend.

"Love can make magic more powerful," Ranelle remarked.

"Mama, it's alright. I'm here." Azura smiled and took her hands.

"Who — who are you?" Lyra shoved her hands away. "Why am I here? I don't know where I am!"

"Easy, Lyra. You're in Varden city — your home." Novia kept her voice gentle.

Thunder boomed overhead.

An outsider came running towards them. "The shield is breaking."

"Gather your people and get everyone inside the palace." Novia motioned towards the building.

"We have to prepare for battle. Once the shield comes down, there'll be nothing standing between us and the Archdruid."

"Shouldn't we search for the queen?" Novia frowned.

"Even if we find her, there's not much we can do to stop her until Nyx and Darius get back."

Together, they herded the Outsiders into the palace. They had Ada take Lyra off to a different chamber so she could rest.

"Time to prepare ourselves for battle."

Novia and Niamh froze as energy jolted through them.

Something is wrong. Nyx… Pain tore through her like a knife through flesh.

She and Niamh slumped to the ground. Their dragons screamed and fell down beside them. Novia appeared standing over her body as a spirit.

"I have Ambrose," Dahlia called out as she dragged the druid into the hall.

"What's happening?" Ranelle cried. "Dahlia, do something."

The Ilari knelt and touched the sisters. "I can't. They're dead."

***

Niamh found herself floating in darkness. Images, memories from her childhood, came flooding back. Playing with her sisters, her bond with her animus, learning things with their father.

All that came back as if a door had opened and she could finally step through. Up until the day they had woken up in their tomb.

Darius' blood had revived Nyx. In turn, it awakened all of them.

She was Niamh, mind whisperer and former assassin. She was Ava, Princess of Andovia. That was still part of her, but wasn't who she was anymore. She was still Niamh. That would never change.

Niamh opened her eyes. It took a moment to come back to herself.

"What are we going to do with them?" Ada asked from somewhere nearby. "How can they be dead? Something terrible must've happened."

She reached down and grabbed her sister's hand. *I'm here.*

Novia blinked at her. *I remember. Everything.*

Me too. Niamh scrambled up and pulled her in for an embrace. She loved her sisters before, but now their bond for much deeper.

Novia clung to her.

"You're awake." Ada gasped.

"You're alive," Dahlia remarked. "But how?"

"Of course we are." Niamh let go of her sister.

Dahlia shook her head. "You dropped dead. I couldn't revive you."

Niamh grimaced. "Nyx died… For a while."

240

"The shield is down. I got Ambrose back," Dahlia told them.

"Help him into one of the chambers. Better yet." Niamh gripped Novia's arm and waved her free hand. Ambrose vanished into a swirl of orbs.

Dahlia gaped at them. "How did you do that?"

"We're different now. We know who and what we are."

I feel… Stronger, Novia remarked.

Me too.

"We need to be ready. The Dragon Guards are on their way here."

"How are we going to take on Dragon Guards?" Bones asked. "There's barely two dozen of us against trained warriors."

"We'll fight them with everything we've got." Niamh leapt to her feet and helped Novia up. The buzz of minds that came towards them intensified. "Be ready!" She scrambled onto Baron's back.

"We are ready." Novia and Andre braced themselves.

The doors burst open as four Dragon Guards swarmed in.

Niamh leapt into the air and kicked two in the head as she hovered over them. Both guards stumbled. Both fired blasts of energy at her.

The other two guards lunged towards Novia.

Niamh grabbed one of them by the throat, and, pushing against his mental shield, let go of her power. Energy shook the air like thunder, knocking them both to the ground.

"Command me, mistress."

"Stop the other guards." Niamh scrambled up. *Novia, use your touch on them!*

They have shields.

Force your way through them. Niamh threw her knives as another guard came towards them and each blade embedded bounced off his armour. Gods, she hoped Nyx would return soon. They were going to need her.

CHAPTER 33

"Why didn't you do anything to save them?" Darius asked the Great Guardian. He could understand Nyx's anger after what she and her sisters had been through.

"I trusted their safety to someone I thought would help. But they were killed before they had the chance to get the girls to safety." The Guardian sighed. "I made a mistake. I know that, but I can't change the past."

"I should go after her." He rose to his feet and hesitated. "Any advice on how to stop my father and the queen?"

"You and Nyx must work together to do that."

So nothing then. He sighed and turned to go.

"Your father has the strength of the immortals on his side. To defeat him, you need to take away that power. Only an immortal can kill another immortal." The Guardian stepped back. "You can rest in the glade. It's secluded and no one will bother you there." She vanished in a flash of light.

His mind raced with more questions as he made his way through the woods. Stopping his father would be impossible whilst he had the power of eleven immortals on his side. Sometimes he wondered if anyone could defeat his father. Fergus had stayed in power a thousand years — longer than any other Archdruid who had come before him. Only having children so he could one day use them as his next vessel. All that power couldn't be contained in one body forever.

Finding out his father had cheated death many times hadn't surprised him. Fergus was the most powerful Archdruid. No doubt Fergus planned to use Darius as his next vessel. That was why he had been trained in druid magic and dark sorcery — unlike his younger siblings.

The trees parted and opened into a small glade.

Nyx sat with her head buried against her knees by a small lake that shimmered like a mirror.

"Are you alright?" He crouched beside her and his hand on her shoulder.

She stiffened. "How can you love a living corpse?"

He bit back a smile. "You're not a corpse. You're still Nyx."

"Am I? Or am I Aerin?" She shook her head. "I feel like I don't know who I am anymore."

"You're still you. That hasn't changed."

"Hasn't it? I don't know who I am. The girl I used to be or the woman I was becoming." Nyx looked up. "I don't know how to deal with this."

"You know who you are. That hasn't changed. You're still the girl I fell in love with."

"We should get back to the old city."

"We will. It's been a long day; we should get some rest. It will be dark soon. It will be easier to travel back to the old city then.

"What about the Dragon Guard?"

"We'll find a way past them. Hopefully, our powers will be recovered by then."

"I can't sleep. I just want to forget everything for a while." She pulled him in for a kiss. "Help me to forget. If we die tomorrow, I want to be with you in every way first. Make love to me."

Darius hesitated. "Are you sure?" She deepened their kiss and pulled him closer.

Darius woke up a few hours later. The sky had turned black. Nyx lay snuggled beside him. Her body entwined with his.

He kissed her. "We should get going."

"Why? Why can't we stay here forever?"

"We both know we can't." He brushed her hair off her face. "You're beautiful."

She snorted. "Not like this I'm not." She wriggled out of his embrace and tossed him his trousers. "Are you sure you feel alright? What if —"

"I'm not enslaved to you." He pulled his trousers back on. "I told you your power wouldn't harm me." He searched around for his fallen shirt and noticed black vines encircling his left wrist. "Holy spirits."

"What — what are those?" Nyx gasped and held up her left arm. Vines circled her wrist in a strange new tattoo. Marked with symbols of fae and druid. Soul bond lines. They were now fully bonded to each other. "How did this happen? I thought we had to say vows to each other."

"Usually you do, but we are bound by blood and magic, so... Us being together would have sealed the bond."

"So we're married now?"

Darius shook his head. "No, a soul bond goes beyond that. Are you sorry that we..."

"Of course not." Nyx's cheek flushed.

He had never wanted this, but he couldn't deny part of him was happy. He took hold of her hands. "I love you more than I thought I could love anyone. I want to be with you. Forever. At least this way we can't be separated."

"Good. I don't ever want to be apart from you again." Nyx wrapped her arms around him.

"See if you can call Ember. We'll need a dragon to get back to the old city."

"I have a better idea." She gripped his hands and orbs of light sparkled around them.

They reappeared in the old palace's great hall.

"It worked." Nyx reached up and gave him a quick kiss. "I feel different now. More powerful."

"We should have access to each other's powers now." Darius let go of her. "Ranelle? Lucien?"

"Sisters!" Nyx yelled.

Niamh and Novia came running in.

"You're alive!" Niamh gasped and threw her arms around Nyx. "Why do you look different?"

"Different how?" Nyx furrowed her brow.

"I don't know… Just different." Niamh scowled. "Don't die on us or run off without us again."

"We died and came back too." Novia gave her a hug.

"Do you remember?" Nyx glanced between her sisters.

"We remember everything." Novia nodded. "Ambrose is here, but we can't wake him."

"I might be able to help with that." Darius headed up to the chamber where Ambrose's body now lay.

He held his hands over Ambrose and chanted something in a mix of the druid tongue and sorcery. He felt different, too. Stronger and much more powerful.

Ambrose gasped as he came awake. His blue eyes opened. "It's good to see you, boy," he rasped.

He squeezed his mentor's shoulder. "You had us all worried, old man."

Nyx and her sisters came in.

"Hello, Father." Niamh scowled.

"Ambrose, we know who you are. Who we are." Nyx crossed her arms. "We remember everything."

Novia looked away. "I still don't understand why you rescued him."

"My girls —" Ambrose rose, then fell back against the bed.

"Don't call us that. We're not your anything," Niamh snapped. "You let us rot in that tomb for a century. Then you kidnapped Novia from Glenfel a couple of months ago." She glanced at Nyx. "Talk to him if you want to, but he can die for all we care." She put a protective arm around Novia and led her out.

"Nyx, I am —"

She shook her head. "Don't. I don't forgive you either. Just tell us how to raise the city shield. There must be another way to control the crystal that powers it. That's the only reason why we saved you."

Pain stabbed through Darius's chest. Ambrose, his betrayal cut her deep. He went over and squeezed her shoulder. He didn't need to say anything. Neither of them needed words.

Ada came in and gave Ambrose food and water.

"The shield can't be raised. Only the queen can activate it," Ambrose said after a few mouthfuls of food.

"Then we'd better find her. We should lock you up next."

All colour drained from Ambrose's face. "Why? I won't hurt anyone."

Nyx didn't look convinced. "Maybe not on purpose, but the queen could still control you."

"She's right." Darius didn't want to lock Ambrose up, but he couldn't deny the threat the other druid proposed.

"The queen can't use me if you release me from her power. Use your touch on me."

Nyx narrowed her eyes. "Why?"

"Because you're the oldest and strongest. Your touch will free me from her."

"Wouldn't you be enslaved to Nyx instead?" Darius frowned.

"No. Use your power so no mind whisperer can touch me. I'll be safe from the queen's control then."

"You'd be safe from my sisters and me, too."

"I'm not your enemy. You know that. I loved you and your sisters more than anything."

She snorted. "I also know you're capable of anything." She grasped Ambrose's throat so hard the druid's eyes bulged. Her power reverberated through the air. "You're free from the queen, but if you ever threaten me or anyone else, I love again, you will die." Ambrose winced, and Darius noted how she forced her words into her power.

She stormed out of the room and he followed after her.

"What was that?" Darius asked. "What did you do to him?"

"I made sure he can't hurt us again. I know you love him like a father, but he is my father and I know him better than anyone."

"I didn't know you could do that." He grimaced, but he couldn't blame her for wanting to protect them all. Ambrose could still pose a threat.

The palace trembled. The Dragon Guard had resumed their attack.

"I'd better find my mother."

"We'll try and hold off the Dragon Guard for as long as we can." He pulled her in for a kiss. "Promise me you'll be careful."

"You be careful too." She gave him one last kiss, then disappeared in a swirl of orbs.

CHAPTER 34

"Remind me again why we need to find our mother,"
Niamh grumbled.

"Because we need an immortal to help get the Archdruid
out of the city," Nyx replied. "You two stay here and help
Darius and the others." She climbed onto Ember's back. "I
won't be long."

"How do you expect to find and overpower her on your
own?" Novia crossed her arms. "Just because we have our
memories back doesn't mean you can convince her to
help."

"Taliesin could have his powers back, too." Niamh's
brow creased. "I don't like this. We should go with you and
watch your back."

"No, stay and keep the Dragon Guard at bay. Ember
and I will be fine."

"But —" Novia protested.

"I have Darius with me — or at least part of him." She
held up her wrist.

"Is that what I think it is?" Niamh's mouth fell open.
"Are they soul bond marks?"

"It's a long story. I'll tell you about it later." Ember took
off and left the palace behind them.

Nyx hoped her sisters would be happy about her news.
She loved Darius. He was a part of her now. The idea of

being together forever didn't frighten her as much as she thought it would.

Head straight for the shield room, she told Ember. *If I know my mother, she would go there if she wanted to hide where no one would find her.*

The question was, what would she do when she found her mother?

Ambrose? She reached out to him with her mind.

Nyx.

I need you to get the queen's body. Take it back to the palace.

Nyx, you can't be thinking of —

Do you have a better way of stopping the Archdruid?

No, but—

Good, then do as I say and don't you dare think of turning against us. Because my magic won't let you.

Ambrose handed the Archdruid the city and turned to him for help in stopping the queen before. Nyx wouldn't let history repeat itself.

If you let your mother regain her power, there's no telling what she'll do to all of you, Ambrose protested.

You asked me to trust you. I'm doing that. Trust me too. I won't let her get her revenge. I know what she'd do. But I'll stop her from doing any further damage.

Ambrose laughed. *You really think you can?*

I'm not a child anymore. She broke the connection to him. They glided over the tree line. Nyx raised her hand and tree branches groaned and creaked as they moved aside to reveal a stone building.

Ember landed on the roof, and Nyx scrambled off him.

My mother must be around here somewhere. She jumped off the roof and Ember followed. If she cast her senses out, Evony would know she was here.

Nyx chanted something in the old druid tongue to conceal them. Light sparkled around her and Ember. It took a few moments for her to remember where the door was.

She pressed her hand against the side of the wall. The door groaned as it slid open. Ember shifted into a wolf and trotted along beside her as she headed through a series of passages. They headed further down the passageway until they reached a dead end. Symbols covered the wall.

"It's been a long time since I've been here." Nyx took a deep breath.

Can you open it?

"I don't know. If I don't get the combination right, it will trigger a trap that will probably kill both of us." She searched her mind for the combination and tapped the different symbols.

Light flashed, and the wall slid open. It amazed her how the combination hadn't changed in the last century. Up ahead loomed a giant crystal that hummed with energy. This had once protected the entire realm, not just the old city.

This is it. But I don't— Nyx ducked as a bolt of energy came at her.

Ember growled.

"Hello, Mother." She rounded a corner and found Taliesin's body slumped against the wall. "You're not looking so well. Did that body not give you what you needed?"

Evony scrambled up. "How did you find me?"

"I'm your daughter, and I remember everything."

"So, why are you here? Come to imprison me again?"

She shook her head. "I came to get you. Ambrose can help put you back in your body."

Taliesin's eyes narrowed. "Why would you do that?"

"Because the Archdruid is here and you're the only one who has enough power to activate the shield. So let's go."

"You expect me to —"

"Believe what you like. We both want the Archdruid gone. So, do you want your body back or not?"

"I'm not a fool, Aerin. I know you'll try something once I'm back inside my body."

"For once, our goals are aligned. You can believe that. And don't call me Aerin, I'm still Nyx."

The queen scowled. "That's not your true name."

"It's who I am. Aerin died a long time ago." She held out her hand.

The queen hesitated, then grasped her fingers. Light sparkled around them as they transported out.

They reappeared outside in the palace courtyard. Overhead, fire exploded and dragons circled everywhere.

Ambrose stood beside a coffin. "I have it."

The queen sneered at Nyx. "Why would you save his worthless hide?"

"Because we need him for this. He was the only one who knew where to find your body." Nyx waved her hand.

The Great Guardian appeared in a swirl of orbs. "Nyx, what are you doing? Why —" She paled. "Evony."

"Hello, Mother." The queen laughed. "How fitting. We are all together again."

Nyx waved her hand, and a collar appeared around the Great Guardian's throat, rendering her powerless.

The Guardian gaped at her. "Nyx, you can't do this."

"Sorry, Guardian, but you owe me and my sisters after what you let happen to us. Ambrose, start the spell."

Ambrose began chanting in the old fae tongue.

Nyx, Evony and the Great Guardian placed their hands on the coffin. Lights swirled between them as he continued chanting.

The queen gasped as her soul left Taliesin's body and the coffin melted away. Slowly the burnt corpse reformed, bathed in golden light.

Part of the palace roof exploded as an enormous black dragon charged towards them, carrying the Archdruid. The Archdruid's dragon landed just as the golden light blinded them all.

Nyx covered her eyes and winced.

One by one, the Dragon Guard, Darius and the others landed a few feet away. Along with Dahlia and the Outsiders.

The light ebbed as a woman stood barefoot. Her long raven hair fell to her waist. Her eyes blazed with purple light and dark purple wings stretched out behind her.

So that's where I get my wings from. Nyx took a step back.

The queen held out her hands. Her pale skin shimmered, and she wore a long black armoured gown. The Morrigan gasped, taking several deep breaths. Her hands went up to her face as she ran them over her flesh.

Taliesin collapsed a few feet away and the Guardian crawled over to him.

Nyx knelt beside them. "Is he alright?"

"He's alive. Nyx, you should never have done this." The Guardian shook her head. "You can't let her staying power. I've seen the destruction she will cause."

"Oh, do shut up, Mother," Evony growled. "You know you can't stop the prophecy and I'm the one who will fulfil it, not Aerin."

"Don't call me Aerin," Nyx snapped.

The Archdruid landed a few feet from them alongside his dragon. "You," the Archdruid snarled.

Fergus raised his hand and a column of fire met the Morrigan's magic head on.

Nyx reached up and tugged at the collar on the Guardian. "It won't come off." Curse it, using this has been an integral part of her plan to stop her mother. If this didn't work, they might not be any way to stop the Morrigan.

Darius rushed over to her. "We don't have much time."

"Help me get this off."

"Maybe you should let them destroy each other," Darius mused.

"Neither can stay in power or they will wage war all over Erthea," the Guardian warned. "Thousands will die."

We need to render to the queen powerless, she told Darius.

Darius tugged at the collar as well then raised his hand. "I'm sorry, Guardian." Lightning burst from up from the earth and the Guardian slumped to the ground.

"What are you doing?" Nyx gasped. "She's immortal, you can't kill an immortal."

"Her power must come from Erthea as well. Don't worry, I only brought her to the point of death." He grappled with the collar and it finally unclasped.

Bursts of light from the warring Archdruid and Morrigan continued to explode around them. Niamh and Novia ducked out of the way as they tried to make their way towards them.

"We need the queen to reinforce the shield. She can't do that with her magic bound," Nyx said.

"Maybe I can help." Darius raised his hand. *When she is distracted, get close to her and put the collar on her.* Lines of energy zigzagged across the ground and formed a web around the Archdruid and knocked him to the ground, containing his magic inside.

"You really think this will hold me, boy?" Fergus snarled.

"You're making this too easy." Evony laughed and hurtled another bolt of energy at the Archdruid.

Nyx went up behind Evony, about to clasp the collar in place. Evony spun around. The collar flew out of Nyx's hands and slammed around her neck instead.

Nyx gasped. No, this couldn't be happening. She needed her powers to stop her mother.

"Don't think I will go down so easily, daughter." Evony shot a bolt of energy towards her.

Nyx screamed as white fire engulfed her, scorching her skin and burning through her wings. She collapsed to the ground, still writhing in pain.

The Dragon Guard continued to fire blasts of dragon fire towards the Morrigan.

"You all need to get out of my city. You're not welcome here." The Morrigan raised her hands and light blazed all around them as the city's shield flared back to life. Screams rang out as one by one all of the Dragon Guards disappeared.

"Don't," Evony said when Darius raised his hand to strike her. "You don't have the power to defeat me. I'm not old and passive like my mother."

Light exploded around the Archdruid as he broke through Darius' web. He stumbled and clutched his stomach. Blood poured from his side from where the queen had struck him. "This isn't over, witch." Fire flashed around him as he vanished in a blaze of flames.

Evony grinned. "You can't save Nyx. With that collar, she's not bound to you anymore."

Darius growled. "I will kill you for this."

Evony laughed. "I'm immortal. You're a mere druid. You'll never stop me. But thanks to you both, I'm back and I will finally have my revenge." Light blazed around her as the queen, Nyx, Taliesin and the Guardian all vanished.

EPILOGUE

"There's no sign of them anywhere in the old city." Darius jumped from Sirin's back as he joined the others in the courtyard. "I can't sense Nyx anymore."

He couldn't believe Nyx had vanished without a trace. Why couldn't he sense her? They had sealed their bond and were fully joined to each other now. Nothing should be able to interfere with that. Not even the Morrigan.

"She can't just vanish." Niamh slid off Baron. "You must be able to sense her."

He shook his head, face grim. "Don't you think I want to? The Morrigan must have blocked it somehow." He ran his fingers over the black vines encircling his left wrist. His last and only connection left to Nyx. "Where would your mother go? If she's not here in Andovia, where?"

Niamh shrugged. "I don't know. I don't pretend to know that woman anymore."

Novia and Andre flew over. "We have been flying all over the realm. The Archdruid's forces suffered a massive blow. The queen didn't just force the Dragon Guard out, she killed almost every guard in the entire realm. The Archdruid and most of his forces have left."

"My father is injured. He won't stay here. He'd go somewhere more protected."

"Where?" Niamh narrowed her eyes.

"Almara maybe — I can't be sure since he is always moving around. With the Queen on the loose he will gather all his power and armies to him. But he will need time to recover. The queen hurt him, and he won't want his enemies seeing him at the time of weakness."

"Andovia has been left under the control of Gideon," Novia told them.

"Why would she take Nyx?" Darius' hands clenched into fists. "Or Taliesin and the Great Guardian?"

"Evony will need to consolidate her power as well." Ambrose came up behind them, staff in hand. "War is coming. Evony won't stop until she gets her revenge and finds the other Twelve."

Darius shook his head. "My father won't allow an immortal to go against him. I'm worried other people might try turning against him now as well if they learn he is weak."

"How do we get Nyx back?" Niamh demanded. "Mother might kill her."

"No, she would have killed her already. No doubt she needs Nyx and her parents in her fight against the Archdruid," Ambrose said. "I promise I'll do everything I can to help you find Nyx."

"With my father weakened, there's never been a better time to strike against him."

"What do you mean?" Niamh frowned.

"I'm going to take Andovia away from him and take my brother prisoner. With war coming, I'm not standing by and doing nothing." He leapt onto Sirin's back. "I'm going to get Nyx back and destroy my father and the queen. Who's with me?"

If you enjoyed this book please leave a review on
Amazon or book site of your choice.

***

For updates on more books and news releases sign
up for my newsletter on tiffanyshand.com/newsletter

ALSO BY TIFFANY SHAND

ANDOVIA CHRONICLES

Dark Deeds Prequel

The Calling

The Rising

Hidden Darkness

Morrigan's Heirs

ROGUES OF MAGIC SERIES

Bound By Blood

Archdruid

Bound By Fire

Old Magic

Dark Deception

Sins Of The Past

Reign Of Darkness

Rogues Of Magic Complete Box Set Books 1-7

ROGUES OF MAGIC NOVELLAS

Wyvern's Curse

Forsaken

On Dangerous Tides

EVERLIGHT ACADEMY TRILOGY

Everlight Academy, Book 1: Faeling

Everlight Academy, Book 2: Fae Born

Hunted Guardian – An Everlight Academy Story

THE FEY GUARDIAN SERIES

Memories Lost

Memories Awakened

Memories Found

The Fey Guardian Complete Series

THE ARKADIA SAGA

Chosen Avatar

Captive Avatar

Fallen Avatar

The Arkadia Saga Complete Series

ABOUT THE AUTHOR

Tiffany Shand is a writing mentor, professionally trained copy editor and copy writer who has been writing stories for as long as she can remember. Born in East Anglia, Tiffany still lives in the area, constantly guarding her workspace from the two cats which she shares her home with.

She began using her pets as a writing inspiration when she was a child, before moving on to write her first novel after successful completion of a creative writing course. Nowadays, Tiffany writes urban fantasy and paranormal romance, as well as nonfiction books for other writers, all available through eBook stores and on her own website.

Tiffany's favourite quote is *'writing is an exploration. You start from nothing and learn as you go'* and it is armed with this that she hopes to be able to help, inspire and mentor many more aspiring authors.

When she has time to unwind, Tiffany enjoys photography, reading, and watching endless box sets. She also loves to get out and visit the vast number of castles and historic houses that England has to offer.

You can contact Tiffany Shand, or just see what she is writing about at:

Author website: tiffanyshand.com

Business site: Write Now Creative

Twitter: @tiffanyshand

Facebook page: Tiffany Shand Author Page